Richmal Crompton was born in Lancashire in 1890. The first story about William Brown appeared in *Home* magazine in 1919, and the first collection of William stories was published in book form three years later. In all, thirty-eight William books were published, the last one in 1970, after Richmal Crompton's death.

'Probably the funniest, toughest children's books ever written'

Sunday Times on the Just William series

*Other books available in the
Just William series*

Just William
More William
William – the Fourth
William at War

William Again

Richmal Crompton

Illustrated by
Thomas Henry

MACMILLAN CHILDREN'S BOOKS

To Tommy

First published 1923
This selection first published 1995 by Macmillan Children's Books

This edition published 2005 by Macmillan Children's Books
a division of Macmillan Publishers Limited
20 New Wharf Road, London N1 9RR
Basingstoke and Oxford
www.panmacmillan.com

Associated companies throughout the world

ISBN 1 405 05459 X

1 3 5 7 9 8 6 4 2

A CIP catalogue record for this book is available from
the British Library

Printed and bound in Great Britain by Mackays of Chatham plc, Kent

CONTENTS

CHAPTER 1

WHAT DELAYED THE GREAT MAN

William, taking his character as a whole, was not of the artistic genre. He had none of the shrinking sensitiveness and delicate imaginativeness of the true artist. But the fact remains that this summer he was impelled by some inner prompting to write a play.

The idea had been growing in his mind for some time. He had seen plays acted by the village amateur dramatic society which was famous more for a touching reliance on the prompter than for any real histrionic talent.

William had considered them perfect. He had decided, after their last performance, to go on the stage. But none of his friends could inform him of the preliminary steps necessary for getting on the stage. It is true that the man in the boot shop, whose second cousin was a scene-shifter in a provincial music-hall, had promised to use his influence, but when William was told the next week that the second cousin had been dismissed for appearing in a state of undeniable intoxication and insisting on accompanying the heroine on to the stage, he felt that all hopes from that direction must be abandoned. It was then that he had the brilliant idea. He would write a play himself and act in that.

William had great confidence in his own powers. He had no doubts whatever of his ability to write a play and act in it. If he couldn't go on *the* stage he'd go on *a* stage. Surely no one could object to that. All he'd want would be some paper and ink and a few clothes. Surely his family – bent as they always were on clouding his moments of purest happiness – couldn't object to that?

'Jus' ink an' paper an' a few ole clothes,' he said wistfully to his mother.

She eyed him with a mistrust that was less the result of a suspicious nature than of eleven years' experience of her younger son.

'Won't pencil do?' she said.

'Pencil!' he said scornfully. 'Did – did Shakespeare or – or the man wot wrote 'The Red Gang' – well, did *they* write in pencil?'

Mrs Brown, having no knowledge of the subject, shifted her point of attack.

'What sort of clothes will you want?' she said.

'Oh – jus' clothes,' said William vaguely.

'Yes, but what sort?'

'How can I tell,' said William irritably, 'till I've *wrote* the play?'

William's family long remembered the silence and peace that marked the next few afternoons. During them, William, outstretched upon the floor of the summer house, wrote his play with liberal application of ink over his person and clothes and the surrounding woodwork. William was not of that class of authors who neglect the needs of the body. After every few words he took a deep draught from a bottle of Orange Ale that stood on his right and a bite from an ink-coated apple on his left. He had laid in a store of apples and sweets and chocolates under the seat of the summer house for his term of authorship. Every now and then he raised a hand to his frowning brow in thought, leaving upon it yet another imprint of his ink-sodden fingers.

'Where is he?' said his father in a hushed wonder at the unwonted peace.

'He's in the summer house writing a play,' said his wife.

'I hope it's a nice long one,' said her husband.

William had assembled his cast and assigned them their parts. Little Molly Carter was to be the heroine, Ginger

3

the hero, Henry the hero's friend, Douglas a crowd of out-laws, William himself was to be the villain, stage-manager and prompter. He handed them their parts with a lofty frown. The parts were in a grimy exercise book.

'It's all wrote out,' he said. 'You jus' learn it where it says your names. Molly's Lady Elsabina—'

'Elsabina isn't a name *I've* ever heard,' said that lady pertly.

'I didn't say it was, did I?' said William coldly. 'I shu'n't be surprised if there was lots of names you'd never heard of. An' Ginger is Sir Rufus Archibald Green an' Henry is the Hon Lord Leopold, an' I'm Carlo Rupino, a villain. All you've gotter do is to learn your parts an' Wednesday morning we'll go through it jus' to practise it, an' Wednesday afternoon we'll do it.'

'We can't three learn out of one book,' said the leading lady, who was inclined to make objections.

'Yes, you *can*,' said William. 'You can take turns sitting in the middle.'

Lady Elsabina sniffed.

'And such writing!' she said scornfully.

'Well, I don't count on my fingers,' said William, returning scorn for scorn, 'not so's everyone can see me, at any rate.'

At which public allusion to her arithmetical powers,

Lady Elsabina took refuge in another sniff, followed by a haughty silence.

The rehearsal was not an unqualified success. The hero-ine, as is the way of heroines, got out of bed the wrong side. After a stirring domestic scene, during which she bit her nurse and flung a basin of bread and milk upon the floor, she arrived tearful and indignant and half an hour late at the rehearsal.

'Can't you come a bit later?' said the stage-manager bitterly.

'If you're going to be nasty to me,' returned the hero-ine stormily, 'I'm going back home.'

'All right,' muttered the stage-manager, cowed, like most stage-managers, by the threatening of tears.

The first item on the agenda was the question of the wardrobe. William had received an unpleasant surprise which considerably lowered his faith in human nature gen-erally. On paying a quiet and entirely informal visit to his sister's bedroom in her absence, to collect some articles of festive female attire for his heroine, he had found every drawer, and even the wardrobe, locked. His sister had kept herself informed of the date of the performance, and had taken measures accordingly. He had collected only a crochet-edged towel, one of the short lace curtains from the window, and a drawn threadwork toilet-cover. Otherwise his search was barren. Passing through the kitchen, however, he found one of her silk petticoats on a clothes horse and added it to his plunder. He found various other articles in other parts of the house. The dressing up took place in an outhouse that had once been a stable at the back of William's house. The heroine's dress consisted of Ethel's silk petticoat with holes cut for the arms. The lace curtain formed an effective head-dress, and the toilet-cover pinned on to the end of the petticoat made a handsome train.

The effect was completed by the crochet-edged towel pinned round her waist. Sir Rufus Archibald Green, swathed in an Indian embroidered table-cover, with a black satin cushion pinned on to his chest, a tea cosy on his head, and an umbrella in his hand, looked a princely hero. The Hon Lord Leopold wore the dining-room tablecloth and the morning-room wastepaper basket with a feather, forcibly wrested from the cock's tail by William, protruding jauntily from the middle. Douglas, as the crowd, was simply attired in William's father's top hat and a mackintosh.

William had quietly abstracted the top hat as soon as he heard definitely that his father would not be present at the performance. William's father was to preside at a political meeting in the village hall, which was to be addressed by a Great Man from the Cabinet, who was coming down from London specially for the occasion.

'Vast as are the attractions of any enterprise promoted by you, William,' he had said politely at breakfast, 'duty calls me elsewhere.'

William, while murmuring perfunctory sorrow at these tidings, hastily ran over in his mind various articles of his father's attire that could therefore be safely utilised. The robing of William himself as the villain had cost him much care and thought. He had finally decided upon the drawing-room rug pinned across his shoulder and a fern-pot upon his head. It was a black china fern-pot and rather large, but it rested upon William's ears, and gave him a commanding and sinister appearance. He also carried an umbrella.

These preparations took longer than the cast had foreseen, and, when finally large moustaches had been corked upon the hero's, villain's and crowd's lips, the lunch-bell sounded from the hall.

'Jus' all finished in time!' said William the optimist.

'Yes, but wot about the rehearsal,' said the crowd gloomily, 'wot about that?'

'Well, you've had the book to learn the stuff,' said William. 'That's enough, isn't it? I don't s'pose real acting people bother with rehearsals. It's quite easy. You jus' learn your stuff an' then say it. It's silly wasting time over rehearsals.'

'Have you learnt wot you say, William Brown?' said the heroine shrilly.

'I *know* wot I say,' said William loftily, 'I don't need to *learn*!'

'William!' called a stern sisterly voice from the house. 'Mother says come and get ready for lunch.'

William merely ejected his tongue in the direction of the voice and made no answer.

'We'd better be taking off the things,' he said, 'so's to be in time for this afternoon. Half past two it begins, then we can have a nice long go at it. Put all the things away careful behind that box so's bothering ole people can't get at them an' make a fuss.'

'William, where *are* you?' called the voice impatiently. The tone goaded William into reply.

'I'm somewhere where *you* can't find me,' he called.

'You're in the stable,' said the voice triumphantly.

'Seems as if folks simply couldn't leave me alone,' said William wistfully, as he removed his fern-pot and fur rug and walked with slow dignity into the house.

'Wash yourself first, William,' said the obnoxious voice.

'I *am* washed,' returned William coldly, as he entered the dining-room, forgetting the presence of a smudgy, corked moustache upon lips and cheeks.

It was an unfortunate afternoon as far as the prospects of a large audience were concerned. Most of the adults of the place were going to listen to the Great Man. Most of the juveniles were going to watch a football match. Moreover, the cast, with the instincts of the very young, had shrouded the enterprise so deeply in mystery in order to enjoy the sensation of superiority, that they had omitted to mention either the exact nature of the enterprise or the time at which it would take place.

On the side-gate was pinned a notice:

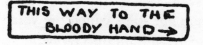

In the stable was a row of old chairs all turned out of the house at various times because of broken backs and legs. As a matter of fact, the cast were little concerned with the audience. The great point was that they were going to act a play – they scarcely cared whether anyone watched it or not. Upon a broken chair in the middle sat a small child, attracted by the notice. Her chair had only lost one leg, so, by sitting well on to one side, she managed to maintain an upright position on it. At a stern demand for money from William, she had shyly slipped a halfpenny into the fern-pot, which served the double purpose of head-gear and pay desk. She now sat – an enthralled spectator – while the cast dressed and argued before her.

Outside down the road came the Great Man. He had come by an earlier train by mistake and was walking slowly towards the village hall, intensely bored by the prospect of the afternoon. He stopped suddenly, arrested by a notice on a side gate:

THIS WAY TO THE BLOODY HAND →

He took out his watch. Half an hour to spare. He hesitated a moment, then walked firmly towards the Bloody Hand. Inside an outhouse a group of curiously dressed children stared at him unsmilingly. One of them, who was dressed in a rug and a fern-pot, addressed him with a stern frown.

INSIDE AN OUTHOUSE A GROUP OF CURIOUSLY DRESSED
CHILDREN STARED AT HIM UNSMILINGLY.

'We're jus' going to begin,' he said, 'sit down.'

The Great Man sat down obediently and promptly collapsed upon the floor.

'You shu'n't have sat on a chair with two legs gone,'

said William impatiently. 'You've broke it altogether now. You can manage all right if you try one with only one gone. We're jus' going to begin.'

The Great Man picked up himself and his hat and sat down carefully upon the farthermost edge of a three-legged chair.

William, holding the mangled remains of an exercise book in his hand, strode forward.

'*The Bloody Hand*, by William Brown,' he announced in a resonant voice.

'Well, an' wot about us?' said the heroine shrilly.

'You didn't write it, did you?' said William. 'I'm only saying who wrote it.'

'Well, aren't you going to say who axe it?' she said pugnaciously.

'No, I'm *not*!' said the stage-manager firmly. 'You jus' say the one wot wrote it. You don't go on saying all them wot axe it.'

'Well, I'm not going to be in it, then,' she said. 'I'm going home.'

William decided to be a woman-hater for the rest of his life.

'All right,' he capitulated, 'if you're going to be so disagreeable – jus' like a girl' – he strode forward again and raised his voice, '*The Bloody Hand*, wrote, every bit of it, by William Brown – acted by Molly Carter an' Ginger an' Douglas an' Henry – they jus' learnt wot William Brown wrote. Now, if you'll be quiet a minute,' he went on to his silent audience, 'we'll begin. You begin,' he said to the damsel in the lace curtain.

She advanced. The rest of them stood in a corner and watched.

'She's *on*,' William announced to the audience. 'We're *off*. Go on!' he repeated to her.

'I'm jus' going to,' she replied irritably, 'soon as you stop talking.' Then, changing her voice to one of shrill artificiality, 'Ho! Where am I? Lorst in a dreadful forest—'

'It's meant to be a forest,' explained the author to the audience.

'I wish you'd stop keep on saying things,' said the heroine. 'I forget where I am. Lorst in a dreadful forest. What shall I do? Ah, me! Crumbs! Who is this who yawns upon my sight?'

'*Dawns!*' corrected the prompter.

'A fierce villain,' went on the heroine, ignoring him, 'methinks. I shouldn't be surprised if it wasn't Carlo Rupino of the Bloody Hand. Oh Lor! What shall I do? Ah me! He draws nearer.'

'It is him,' prompted William.

'I was jus' going to say that, if you wouldn't keep on

interrupting. It is him. I was jus' going to say it. Ah me!
What shall I do? Whither shall I flee? Nowhere. Gadzooks!
He draws nearer.'

'I come on now,' explained William to the audience,
holding on to his fern-pot with one hand to steady it. 'I'm
him.' He advanced threateningly upon the maiden. 'Aha!'
he sneered. 'Gadzooks! Doest thou happen to know who I
am?'

'I am lorst in the dreadful forest,' she replied. 'Ah me!
What shall I do?'

'I am Carlo Rupino of the Bloody Hand. Go on, *faint*!'
he urged in an undertone.

''F you think I'm going to faint on this dirty ole floor,'
she replied, 'I'm jus' not. You should have brushed it up a
bit 'f you wanted me to faint on it.'

'You don't know how to,' he jeered.

'I *do*! I *can*! I can faint beautifully on our drawing-
room carpet. I'm jus' not going to faint on a dirty ole
stable floor an' I'm not going to be *in* your nasty ole play
'f you're not going to be nice to me.'

'All right, then, don't be. You jus' take off my sister's
petticoat, an' our lace curtain an' don't be in it, if you
don't want to be.'

'Well, I jus' *won't*, if you're going on like this at me.'

'Well, 'f you keep on talkin' not out of the play who's

to know when you're talkin' play an' when you're jus'
talkin' yourself?'

'Anyone with any sense could—'

'Oh, get on with it,' said the hero off the scenes. 'You'll
never get to where I come in, if you're going on like this all
day. *Pretend* she's fainted and go on from there.'

'All right,' said the villain obligingly. 'Aha! I hast thee
in my power. I wilt hang thee ere dawn dawns from my
remote mountain lair.' The toilet-cover train caught on a
nail and the petticoat tore with an echoing sound. 'That's
right,' he went on, 'go on messin' up my sister's things,
so's she'll never be able to wear them again.'

''F you're going to keep on being nasty to me,' said the
heroine again, 'I'm going straight back home an' I'm not
going to be *in* your ole play.'

'Well, anyway,' said William, with a mental determination that his next play should contain no heroines,
'now we go off and they come on.'

The hero and his friend advanced.

'Alas!' said Sir Rufus Archibald Green, 'I see no trace of
her. What canst have happened to her? I hope she hast not
met yon horrible ole villain, Carlo Rupino, of the Bloody
Hand. Seest thou any footmarks of her, the Hon Lord
Leopold?'

The Hon Lord Leopold examined the stable floor.

'Lookin' for footmarks,' explained the stage-manager to the audience.

'Ah me! None!' said the Hon Lord Leopold. Then, looking more closely. 'Crikey! Yes!' he said. 'I seest footmarks. 'Tis hers and Carlo Rupino's. I knowest their boots.'

'Ah me!' said the hero. 'What cattastrop is here? Gadzooks! Let us follow to his remote mountain lair. I will kill him dead and cut out his foul black heart and put an end to his foul black life.'

He waved Mrs Brown's best umbrella threateningly as he spoke. 'Now they come off,' explained William, 'an' we come on. Here's the gallows.'

He carried forward a small reading stand, taken from his father's study, then advanced holding the hand of the fair Elsabina. The crowd in his top hat and mackintosh stood in attendance.

'Aha!' said Carlo Rupino to his victim. 'I hast thee in my power, thou ole girl! I am now going to hang thee from yon lofty gallows! Go on!' he addressed the crowd.

The crowd took off his top hat and uttered a feeble 'Hurray!'

'You couldn't hang me from that old thing,' remarked the heroine scornfully.

'That's not in the play,' said William.

'I know it isn't. I'm just saying that myself.'

'Well, say wot's in the play.'

At that point the chair, upon which the Great Man was with difficulty sitting, collapsed suddenly, precipitating the Great Man among its fragments. William turned upon him sternly.

' 'F you're going to keep on making noises breaking chairs,' he said, 'how d'you think we're going to get on?'

The Great Man raised himself from the debris with a murmured apology, brushed himself as well as he could, and sat down quietly upon an adjacent packing-case.

'Well, go on!' said William to the heroine.

'Something about "Oh, mercy, spare me!" an' then I've forgot what comes after that.'

'Well, why didn't you learn it?'

'I can't read your nasty old writing – all blots an' things spilt on it.'

'Well, you can't write a play at all, so you needn't go making remarks about people's writing what can.'

'Oh, go on!' said the egotistical hero off the stage. 'Let's get to where I come on.'

William studied his exercise book carefully.

'Here's wot you say,' he said. ' "Oh, mercy, spare me—" '

'I said that.'

'Be quiet! "Oh, mercy, spare me—"'

'I *said* that.'

'Be *quiet*! "Oh, mercy, spare me an' let me return to my dear ole mother an' father an' the young gentleman wot I'm going to marry. His name is Sir Rufus Archibald Green." That's wot you say.'

'Well, you've said it, so I needn't say it all over again.'

''F you think I'm going to say all your stuff for you—' began William.

Elsabina, bored with the question, pointed an accusing finger at the Great Man.

'Look at him!' she said. 'He's come in without paying any money.'

Overcome by embarrassment, the Great Man hastily took out a case and handed a ten-shilling note to William. A half-crown would have won rapturous gratitude. A ten-shilling note was beyond their ken. The entire cast gathered round it.

'It's paper money,' said Douglas, impressed.

'I don't suppose it's *real*,' said William gloomily. 'Well, where're we got to?'

He turned quickly, and the fern-pot descended, sharply, extinguishing his head. He struggled with it without success.

'Can't anyone do anything?' said his muffled voice

from inside the fern-pot. 'I can't go on acting like this – people can't *see* me. Well, isn't anyone going to *do* anything?'

The cast pulled without success.

'I didn't say pull my head off,' said the stern, sarcastic voice from inside the pot, 'I said pull the *thing* off!'

The Great Man arose from his packing-case and came to the rescue. Finally William's face appeared. William put his hands to his head. 'Any one'd think you wanted to pull my nose an' ears off – the way you did it,' he said. 'Now let's get on.' He turned to the heroine. '"No, I will not spare thee. I hatest thy mother and thy father and the young gentleman thou ist going to marry. Thy mother, thy father, and the young gentleman thou ist going to marry wilt see they lifeless body dangling on my remote mountain lair ere dawn dawns. Gadzooks!" Now go on! Scream!'

The heroine screamed.

The crowd took off his top hat and cheered.

'"I will keep thee in a deep, dark dungeon, with all sorts of rats an' things crawling about till even, and then – and then—"' He consulted his exercise book, '"and then I'll" – I've forgot this bit, and I can't read wot comes next—'

'*Yah!*' yelled the heroine in shrill triumph.

19

'Shut up!' retorted William. 'Now, you come on,' to the hero. 'Let's do the rest as quick as we can. I'm getting a bit tired of it. Let's go down to the pond an' race boats when we've done.'

'Golly! Yes – *let's*!' said the crowd enthusiastically.

'Girls won't be allowed,' said William to Elsabina. Elsabina elevated her small nose.

' 'S if I wanted to sail *boats*!' she said scornfully.

William's father entered the house hastily.

'Surely the meeting isn't over, dear?' said William's mother.

'He hasn't come,' said Mr Brown. 'Everybody's waiting. We met the train, but he wasn't on it. The station-master says that he came by an earlier one and walked up, but no one can find him. He must have lost his way.'

'William seems to have collected an old tramp in the stable,' said Mrs Brown; 'he may have seen him on the road.'

'I'll go and see,' said Mr Brown.

In the stable a fight was going on between his son in a fur rug and his son's friend in a tablecloth and a tea cosy. Upon both faces were the remains of corked moustaches. A broken fern-pot and a battered top hat were on the

'THOU BEASTLY OLE ROBBER,' DOUGLAS WAS SHOUTING. 'I
WILL KILL THEE DEAD AND CUT OUT THY FOUL, BLACK
HEART.'

floor. Another boy in a mackintosh and a little girl in a
lace curtain were watching.

'Thou beastly ole robber,' Douglas was shouting, 'I
will kill thee dead and cut out thy foul, black heart.'

'Nay!' yelled his son. 'I will hang thee from my mountain ere dawn dawns and thy body shall dangle from the
gallows—'

A wistful-looking old man on a packing-case was an
absorbed spectator of the proceedings. When he saw

William's father he took out his watch with a guilty start.

'Surely—' he said. 'I'd no idea – *Heavens*!'

He picked up his hat and almost ran.

The Great Man rose to address his audience.

'Ladies and gentlemen – I must begin by apologising for my late arrival,' he said with dignity. 'I have been unavoidably delayed.'

He tried not to meet William's father's eye as he made the statement.

CHAPTER 2

THE CURE

Breakfast was not William's favourite meal. With his father shut off from the world by his paper, and his mother by her letters, one would have thought that he would have enjoyed the clear field thus left for his activities. But William liked an audience – even a hostile one consisting of his own family. True, Robert and Ethel, his elder brother and sister, were there; but Robert's great rule in life was to ignore William's existence. Robert would have preferred not to have had a small freckled, snub-nosed brother. But as Fate had given him such a brother, the next best thing was to pretend that he did not exist. On the whole, William preferred to leave Robert alone. And Ethel was awful at breakfast – quite capable of summoning the Head of the Family from behind his *Daily Telegraph* when William essayed a little gentle teasing. This morning William, surveying his family in silence in the intervals of making a very hearty meal, came to the conclusion, not for the first time, that they were hardly worthy of him: Ethel, thinking she was so pretty in that

23

stuck-up-looking dress, and grinning over that letter from that soft girl. Robert talking about football and nobody listening to him, and glaring at him (William) whenever he tried to tell him what nonsense he was talking about it. No, it *wasn't* rounders he was thinking of – he knew 'bout football, thank you, he just did. His mother – suddenly his mother put down her letter.

'Great-Aunt Jane's very ill,' she said.

There was a sudden silence. Mr Brown's face appeared above the *Daily Telegraph*.

'Um?' he said.

'Great-Aunt Jane's very ill,' said Mrs Brown. 'They don't seem to think there's much chance of her getting better. They say—' She looked again at the letter as if to make quite sure: 'They say she wants to see William. She's never seen him, you know.'

There was a gasp of surprise.

Robert voiced the general sentiment.

'Good Lord!' he said. 'Fancy anyone wanting to see *William*!'

'When they're dying, too,' said Ethel in equal horror. 'One would think they'd like to die in peace, anyway.'

'It hardly seems fair,' went on Robert, 'to show William to anyone who's not strong.'

William glared balefully from one to the other.

'Children! Children!' murmured Mrs Brown.

'How,' said Mr Brown, 'are you going to get William over to Ireland?'

'I suppose,' said Mrs Brown, 'that someone must take him.'

'Good Lord! Who?'

'Yes, who?' echoed the rest of the family.

'I can't possibly leave the office for the next few weeks,' said Mr Brown hastily.

'I simply couldn't face the crossing alone – much less with William,' said Ethel.

'I've got my finals coming up next year,' said Robert. 'I don't want to waste any time. I'm working rather hard these vacs.'

'No one,' said his father politely, 'would have noticed it.'

'I can go alone, *thank* you,' said William with icy dignity.

In the end William and Mrs Brown crossed to Ireland together.

'If William drops overboard,' was Robert's parting shot, 'don't worry.'

The crossing was fairly eventful. William, hanging over the edge of the steamer, overbalanced, and was rescued from a watery grave by one of the crew who caught him by his trousers as the overbalancing occurred. William was far from grateful.

'Pullin' an' tuggin' at me,' he said, 'an' I was all right. I was only jus' lookin' over the edge. I'd have got back all right.'

But the member of the crew made life hideous for Mrs Brown.

'You know, lady,' he muttered, 'when I saved yer little boy's life, I give myself such a wrench. I can feel it in my innards now, as it were—'

Hastily she gave him ten shillings. Yet she could not stem the flow.

'I 'ope, lady,' he would continue at intervals, 'when that choild's growd to be a man, you'll think sometoimes of the poor ole man wot saved 'is life at the expense of 'is own innards, as you might say, when 'e were a little 'un.'

A speech like that always won half a crown. In the end Mrs Brown spent her time avoiding him and fleeing whenever she saw him coming along the deck. When a meeting was inevitable she hastily gave him the largest coin she could find before he could begin on his 'innards'.

Meanwhile a passenger had discovered William neatly balanced through a porthole, and earned his undying hatred by hauling him in and depositing him upside down on the floor.

'Seems to me,' said William to his mother, 'that all these folks have come for is to stop other folks having a good time. What do you come on a boat for if you can't look at the sea – that's all I want to know?'

A gale rose, and Mrs Brown, pale and distraught, sat huddled up on deck. William hovered round sympathetically.

'I got some chocolate creams in my other coat. Like some of them?'

'William, dear, don't bother to stay here. I'd just as soon you went away and played.'

'Oh no,' said William nobly. 'I wun't leave you feelin' bad.'

The boat gave a lurching heave. Mrs Brown groaned.

'Think you goin' to *be* sick, Mother?' said William with interest.

'I – I don't know . . . Wouldn't you like to go over to the other side for a change?'

William wandered away. Soon he returned, holding in his hands two doughnuts – masses of yellowy, greasy-looking dough, bearing the impress of William's grimy fingers.

'I've got us one each,' said William cheerfully. 'You must be awful hungry, Mother.'

Mrs Brown gave one glance and turned towards the sea.

In Great-Aunt Jane's drawing-room were assembled Uncle

SOON WILLIAM RETURNED, HOLDING IN HIS HANDS TWO
DOUGHNUTS.

John and Aunt Lucy and Cousin Francis. Francis was about the same age as William, but inordinately fat and clad in white. He had fair curls and was the apple of his parents' eyes. They had heard of William but none of them had seen him. There was a murmur of excitement as the sound of the taxi was heard, then William and his mother entered. Mrs Brown was still pale. William followed her, scowling defiantly at the world in general.

'If you have any brandy—' said Mrs Brown faintly.

'Brandy?' said William cheerfully. 'I never thought of that. I got you nearly everything else, didn't I? I wanted to tempt her to eat,' he explained to the company. 'I thought of choc'lates an' cakes an' cocoa an' pork pies – I *kept* askin' her to try pork pie – there was some lovely ones on the boat – but I never thought of brandy. Have a good drink of it, Mother,' he encouraged her, 'an' then try an' have a go at the chocolates.'

Mrs Brown shivered slightly and sipped the brandy.

'This, William,' said Aunt Lucy, 'is your cousin Francis.'

Cousin Francis held out his hand. 'How do you do, William?'

William took the proffered hand. 'How do you do?' he said loudly, and added *sotto voce*, 'Fatty.'

Thus was war declared.

Mrs Brown was feeling better.

'How is Great-Aunt Jane?' she said.

'Sinking,' said Uncle John in a voice of deepest gloom. 'Sinking fast – sinking fast.'

William's expression grew animated.

'Where is she?' he said. 'Is she out in the sea?'

'Little boys,' said Uncle John still gloomily, 'should be seen and not heard.'

At this point the nurse entered.

'She can see the little boy now,' she said, 'if he's come.'

'Let the dear children go together,' suggested Aunt Lucy.

'Excellent,' said Uncle John in his hushed, sepulchral voice. 'Excellent – together.'

William and Francis went upstairs behind the nurse.

The bedroom was large and dim. At the far end lay Great-Aunt Jane, propped up in a high old-fashioned bed. The nurse took them across.

'I only wanted to see William,' said Great-Aunt Jane feebly. 'The other need not have come. So this is Margaret's youngest, is it? I've seen the others, Robert and Ethel. But I hadn't seen this one. I didn't want to die without seeing all my family. He's not as beautiful as Francis, but he's less fat. Do you trail clouds of glory, William? Francis trails clouds of glory.'

'Clouds of fat more like,' said William, who was beginning to be bored by the whole affair. Great-Aunt Jane closed her eyes.

'I'm going to rest a little,' she said. 'You can stay here and get me anything I want while nurse goes to have her tea.'

The nurse went.

Great-Aunt Jane fell asleep.

William and Francis were left alone in the dim bedroom, sitting on chairs, one on each side of the big bed as the nurse had placed them. The silence grew oppressive. William fidgeted, then opened hostilities.

'Hello, Fatty!' he whispered over Great-Aunt Jane's recumbent form.

' 'F you call me that again,' whispered Francis, 'I'll tell my mother.'

' 'F you went telling tales of me, I'd pull your long hair off.'

Francis searched in his mind, silent for a few minutes, for a suitable term of opprobrium.

'Freckles!' he hissed across the bed at last.

'Softy!' returned William.

This was warfare after his own heart.

' 'F I got hold of you I could throw you out of the window.'

31

'You couldn't. You'd just roll about. You couldn't throw anything. You're too fat.'

'I told you what I'd do if you called me that again.'

'Tell-tale! Tell-tale! Silly ole tell-tale!'

Still the deadly insults were being hurled across the bed in whispers, and still Great-Aunt Jane slept.

'I could bash your old freckled face in,' whispered Francis.

'I could knock your ole long-haired head off.'

'I could pull your ears off.'

'Come on, then. Have a try.'

'Come on yourself!'

Worked up to fighting pitch, they stole round their corners of the bed to the open space at the foot. Then they hurled themselves upon each other.

They fought with fierce satisfaction, tearing at each other's hair, punching each other's heads, squirming and rolling on the floor. Suddenly they became aware of a spectator. Great-Aunt Jane was sitting up in bed, her cheeks flushed, her eyes bright.

'Go it, William!' she said. 'Get one in on his nose. That's right, Fatty; well fended! Go on, William. Another, another! No biting, Fatty. Go— Oh, dear!'

There were footsteps on the stairs.

'Quick!' said Great-Aunt Jane.

They darted to their seats, smoothing their hair as they went.

The nurse entered.

'Whatever—' she began, then looked round the peaceful

'GO IT, WILLIAM!' GREAT-AUNT JANE CRIED . . . !
'ANOTHER, ANOTHER!' . . .

room. 'Oh, it must have been in the street!'

Great-Aunt Jane opened her eyes.

'I feel much better,' she said. '*Ever* so much better.'

'You *look* better,' said the nurse. 'I hope the children were good.'

'Good as gold!' said Great-Aunt Jane, with the ghost of a wink at William.

'Look at them,' said the nurse, smiling. 'Both purple in the face with holding their breaths. They'd better go now.'

Again Great-Aunt Jane winked at William. Downstairs Uncle John was standing, gloomy as ever, by the fireplace.

'How is she?' he said, as they entered.

'I think she's risin' a bit,' said William.

'What did you say he did this morning?' said Great-Aunt Jane to the nurse.

'He got up early,' said the nurse, 'and found a mouse in the mousetrap. He put it into a cardboard box and almost covered the creature in cheese, and made holes in the lid and put it into his pocket. He wanted to keep it. Then the thing gnawed its way out at breakfast and stampeded the whole table. It ran over Francis, and he yelled, and his father nearly fainted. William was much annoyed. He said he'd meant to teach it tricks.'

'It was yesterday, wasn't it,' said Great-Aunt Jane, 'that

he dared Fatty to walk on the edge of the rain tub, and he overbalanced and fell in?'

'Yes – and Fatty got in a temper and bit him, and they fought and rolled down the bank together into the pond.'

'And Tuesday—'

'Tuesday he brought the scarecrow in from the field in the evening and put it in front of the fire where his uncle usually stands, and it was rather dark, and they hadn't lit up yet, and his aunt came in and talked to it for quite a long time before she discovered. She's rather short-sighted, you know.'

'There was a terrible scuffle going on somewhere last night,' said Great-Aunt Jane eagerly.

'Oh, yes – his Uncle John went downstairs about eleven for a book he'd forgotten, and William heard him and thought he was a burglar, and attacked him from behind. They fell downstairs on top of each other, and then William got his uncle rolled up in the hall rug with a pair of gloves in his mouth and his eyeglasses broken before he found out who he was – he's a curious boy!'

Great-Aunt Jane was sitting up and looking quite bright.

'He certainly lends an interest to life. I feel ever so much better since he came. You might send him up now, if he's in, Nurse, will you?'

On her way down the nurse met Uncle John.

'How long is this young ruffian going to be here?' he said furiously. William had successfully dispelled the air of hallowed gloom from the house. 'He's sent my nerves to

'THERE WAS A TERRIBLE SCUFFLING GOING ON
SOMEWHERE, LAST NIGHT.'

pieces already – what his effect on that poor sufferer must be—'

'He seems to be strengthening *hers*,' said the nurse. 'She's just sent for him.'

'That means a few minutes' peace for the rest of the house, at any rate,' he said.

William entered the sickroom sullenly. He was thoroughly bored with life. Even his enemy, Fatty, was not to be found. Fatty retired every afternoon with his mother to lie down.

'Good afternoon, William,' said Great-Aunt Jane, 'are you enjoying your visit?'

'Well,' said William vaguely, striving to temper truth with politeness, 'I wun't mind going home now. I've had enough.' He sat down on her bed and became confidential. 'We've been here for weeks an' weeks—'

'Four days,' amended Great-Aunt Jane.

'Well, four days, then,' said William, 'an' there's nothing left to do, an' they make a fuss if I make a noise; an' I've got a lizard in a box at home and I'm tryin' to teach it tricks, an' it'll have forgot me if I stay here much longer. It was just gettin' to know me. I could tell by its eyes. An' they might forget to feed it or *anything* – there's nothing to *do* here, an' Mother's not been well since the sea made her sick, an' I keep sayin' – why wait till she's all right to go back – case the sea makes her sick again; better go back while she's feelin' bad and get it all over again without the fuss of gettin' all right an' then gettin' bad again; an' I keep sayin', *why* are we stoppin' here and stoppin' here an' stoppin' here – an' everyone sayin' "*Shh!*" when you make a noise, or sing, or anything. I say – *why?*'

Great-Aunt Jane's sunken lips were quivering, her eyes twinkling.

'And why are you stoppin' an' stoppin' an' stoppin'?'

'She says 'cause you're not out of danger, and we must stop till we know which way it is. Well,' he waxed still more confidential, 'what I say is, shurely you *know* which way you're goin' to be. Can't you tell us? Then if you're goin' to get better we'll go, an' if you're not—'

'Yes, what then?' said Great-Aunt Jane.

'Then we'll go, too. You don't want me hangin' round when you're dyin',' he said coaxingly. 'I'd like as not make a noise, or something, and disturb you – and that lizard might have got out if I go waitin' here much more – like wot that mouse did.'

Great-Aunt Jane drew a deep breath of utter content.

'You're too priceless to be true, William,' she said.

'Can't you tell me which way?' said William ingratiatingly.

'Yes,' said Great-Aunt Jane, 'I'm going to get better.'

'Oh, crumbs!' he said joyfully. 'Can I go and tell Mother to pack?'

'You've turned the corner,' said the doctor to Great-Aunt Jane an hour later. 'We needn't worry about you any more. All these relations of yours can pack up and go.'

'William's packed already,' said the nurse. 'That boy is a cure!'

Great-Aunt Jane laughed.

'Yes, he's a cure, all right,' she said.

CHAPTER 3

THAT BOY

William had gone away with his family for a holiday, and he was not enjoying it. For one reason it was not the sea. Last summer they had gone to the sea and William had enjoyed it. He had several times been rescued from a watery grave by passers-by. He had lost several pairs of new shoes and socks by taking them off among the rocks and then roaming so far afield barefoot that he forgot where he had left them and so came home without them. He got wet through every day as a matter of course. Through the house where his family stayed his track was marked by a trail of sand and seaweed and small deceased crabs. He had upon one occasion floated out to sea in a boat which he had found on the beach and loosened from its moorings, and narrowly escaped being run down by a steamer. At the end of the holiday by the sea Mrs Brown had said weakly, 'Let it be somewhere inland next year.'

William found things monotonous inland. There were no crabs and nothing to do. Robert and Ethel, his grown-up brother and sister, had joined a tennis club and were out all day. Not that William had much use for Robert and Ethel. He preferred them out all day as a matter of fact.

'All I say *is*,' he said aggrievedly to his mother, 'that no one cares whether I'm havin' a nice time or not. You think that s'long as father can go golfin' – or *tryin*' to golf – and those two playin' tennis – or what they *call* tennis' – he added scornfully, 'and you can sit knittin', it's all *right*. You don't think of *me*. No one thinks of me. I might just as well not be here. All I say *is*,' he ended, 'I might jus' as well be *dead* for all the trouble some people take to make me happy.'

His mother looked at his scowling freckled countenance.

'Well, dear,' she said, 'there are plenty of books about the house that you haven't read.'

'*Books*,' said William scornfully. 'Sir Walter Scott's ole things – I don't call that *books*.'

'You can go for walks.'

'*Walks!*' said William. 'It's no use goin' walks without Jumble.'

His father lowered his newspaper. 'Your arithmetic report was vile,' he said. 'You might occupy your time with a few sums. I'll set them for you.'

William turned upon his parent a glance before which

most men would have quailed. Even William's father, inured as he was by long experience to that glare of William's, retired hastily behind his paper. Then, with a short and bitter laugh, William turned on his heel and left the room. That was the last straw. He'd finished with them. He'd simply finished with them.

He put his head in at the window as he went towards the gate.

'I'm goin' out, Mother,' he said in a voice which expressed stern sorrow rather than anger.

'All right, dear,' said Mrs Brown sweetly.

'I may not be coming back – never,' he added darkly.

'All right, dear,' said William's mother.

William walked with slow dignity down to the gate.

'All I say *is*,' he remarked pathetically to the gatepost as he passed, 'I might as well be *dead* for all anyone thinks of tryin' to make my life a bit happier.'

He walked down to the village – a prey to black dejection. What people came away for holidays *for* beat him. At home there was old Jumble to take for a walk and throw sticks for, and the next-door cat to tease and the butcher's boy to fight, and various well-known friends and enemies to make life interesting. Here there was – well, all he said *was*, he might as well be *dead*.

A charabanc stood outside the post office, and people

were taking their places in it. William looked at it contemptuously. He began to listen in a bored fashion to the conversation of two young men.

'I'm awfully glad you ran down,' one of them was saying to the other; 'we can have a good tramp together. To tell you the truth I'd got so bored that I'd taken a ticket for this charabanc show . . . Can't stand 'em really.'

'Will they give you your money back?' said the other.

'It doesn't matter,' said the first.

Then he met William's dark, unflinching gaze and said carelessly, 'Here, kid, like a ticket for the charabanc trip?'

William considered the question. Anything that would take him away from the immediate vicinity of his family seemed at that moment desirable.

'Does it come back?' he said.

'It's *supposed to*,' said the young man.

That seemed rather a drawback. William felt that he would have preferred to go away from his family on something that did not come back. However, this was better than nothing.

'All right,' he said graciously, 'I don't mind going.'

The young man handed him the ticket.

William sat in the middle of a seat between a very fat lady and a very fat gentleman.

'Not much *room*,' he remarked bitterly to the world in general.

The fat lady and the fat gentleman turned crushing glances upon him simultaneously. William received and returned them. He even enlarged upon his statement.

'All I say *is*,' he said pugnaciously, trying to scowl up at both sides at once, 'that there's not much *room*.'

The fat lady put up lorgnettes and addressed the fat gentleman over William's head.

'What a very rude little boy!' she said.

Being apparently agreed upon that point they became friendly and conversed together for the rest of the journey, ignoring the subterranean rumbles of indignation that came from the small boy between them.

At last the charabanc stopped at a country village. The driver explained that the church was an excellent example of Early Norman architecture. This left William cold. He did not even glance at it. The driver went on to remark that an excellent meal could be obtained at the village inn. Here William's expression kindled into momentary animation only to fade again into despair. For William had spent his last twopence that morning upon a stick of liquorice. It had caused a certain amount of friction between himself and his elder brother. William had put it – partially sucked – upon a chair while he went to

'ALL I SAY IS.' WILLIAM SAID PUGNACIOUSLY, TRYING TO
SCOWL UP AT BOTH SIDES AT ONCE, 'THAT THERE'S NOT
MUCH *ROOM*.'

wash his hands, and Robert had come in from tennis and
inadvertently sat down upon it. Being in a moist condition
it had adhered to Robert's white flannel trousers. Even
when detached the fact of its erstwhile adherence could
not be concealed. William had considered Robert's attitude entirely unreasonable.

'Well, I don't know what he's got to be mad about . . . I didn't make him sit down on it, did I? He talks about me spoilin' his trousers – well, wot about him spoilin' my liquorice? All I say *is* – who wants to eat it, now he's been sittin' on it?'

Robert had unkindly taken this statement at its face value and thrown the offending stick of liquorice into the fire.

William sadly extricated himself from the charabanc, thinking bitterly of the vanished twopence, and liquorice, and the excellent meal to be obtained from the village inn. He regarded himself at that moment as a martyr whose innocence and unjust persecution equalled that of any in the pages of the Church History book.

An elderly lady in *pince-nez* looked at him pityingly.

'What's the matter, little boy?' she said. 'You look unhappy.'

William merely smiled bitterly.

'Is your mother with you?' she went on.

'Nope,' said William, thrusting his hands into his pockets and scowling still more.

'Your father, then?'

'Huh!' said William, as though bitterly amused at the idea.

'You surely haven't come alone?' said the lady.

William gave vent to the dark emotions of his soul.

'All I say *is*,' he said, 'that if you knew my family you'd be jolly glad to go anywhere alone if you was me.'

The lady made little clicking noises with her tongue expressive of sorrow and concern.

'Dear, dear, dear!' she said. 'And are you going to have tea now?'

William assumed his famous expression of suffering patience.

'I've got no money. It's not much use goin' to have tea anywhere when you haven't got no money.'

'Haven't they given you any money for your tea?' said the lady indignantly.

'Not *they*!' said William with a bitter laugh.

'*They* wun't of let me come if they'd known. *They* wun't of paid anything for me. It was a frien' gave me the ticket jus' to giv' me a bit of pleasure,' he said pathetically, 'but *they* wun't even give me money for my tea.'

'Perhaps,' said the lady, 'you had a late lunch and they thought—'

'Huh!' ejaculated William. 'I din' have *any* lunch worth speakin' of.' He thrust aside the mental picture of two helpings of steak and three of rice pudding.

'You *poor* child,' said the lady. 'Come along, *I'll* give you your tea.'

'Thanks,' said William humbly and gratefully, trudging off with her in the direction of the village inn.

He felt torn between joy at the immediate prospect of a meal and pity for his unhappy home life. William, generally speaking, had only to say a thing to believe it. He saw himself now as the persecuted victim of a cruel and unsympathetic family, and the picture was not without a certain pleasure. William enjoyed filling the centre of the stage in any capacity whatsoever.

'I suppose,' said the lady uncertainly, as William consumed boiled eggs with relish, 'that your family are *kind to you*.'

'You needn't s'pose that,' said William, his mouth full of bread and butter, his scowling gaze turned on her lugubriously. 'You jus' needn't s'pose that. Not with *my* family.'

'They surely aren't *cruel* to you?' said the lady in horror.

'*Crule*,' said William with a shudder, 'jus' isn't the word. All I say *is*, crule isn't the word.'

The lady leant across the table.

'Little boy,' she said soulfully, 'you must tell me *all*. I want to *help* you. I go about the world helping people, and I'm going to help you. Don't be frightened. You know people can be put in prison for being cruel to children. If

I reported the case to the Society for Prevention of Cruelty to Children—'

William was slightly taken back.

'Oh, I wun't like you to do that!' he said hastily. 'I wun't like to get them into trouble.'

'Ah,' she said, 'but you must think of your happiness, not theirs!'

She watched, fascinated, as William finished a third plate of bread and butter, and yet his hunger seemed to be

'LITTLE BOY,' SHE SAID SOULFULLY, 'YOU MUST TELL ME ALL . . . IF I REPORTED THE CASE TO THE SOCIETY FOR PREVENTION OF CRUELTY TO CHILDREN—'

unappeased. She was not acquainted with the digestive capacity of an average healthy boy of eleven.

'I can see you've been starved,' she said, 'and I could tell at once from your expression that you were unhappy. Have you any brothers and sisters?'

William, who had now reached the second stage of his tea, put half a cake into his mouth, masticated and swallowed it before replying.

'Two,' he said briefly. 'One each. Grown-up. But they jus' care nothin' but their own pleasure. Why,' he went on warming to his theme, 'this morning I bought a few sweets with jus' a bit of money I happened to have, an' he took them from me and threw them into the fire. Jus' threw them into the fire.'

The lady made the sympathetic clicking sound with her tongue.

'Dear! Dear! Dear!' she said again. 'How very unkind!'

William somewhat reluctantly refused the last piece of cake. He had, as a matter of fact, done full justice to the excellent meal provided by the village inn. It had given him a feeling of gentle, contented melancholy. He was basking in the thought of his unhappy home life.

'I'm sorry to keep reminding you of it,' said the lady, 'but I feel I really want to get to the bottom of it. There's generally only one explanation of an unhappy home. I've investigated so many cases. Does your father drink?'

William nodded sadly.

'Yes,' he said. 'That's it.'

'Oh,' breathed the lady, 'your *poor* mother!'

But William wanted no division of sympathy.

'Mother drinks, too,' he said.

'You *poor*, poor child!' said the lady.

William wondered whether to make Robert and Ethel drink too, then decided not to. As an artist he knew the value of restraint.

'Never mind,' said the lady, 'you shall have *one* happy afternoon, at any rate.'

She took him to the village shop and bought him chocolates, and sweets, and bananas, and a top. William found some difficulty in retaining an expression suggestive of an unhappy home life, but he managed it fairly successfully.

He began to feel very sleepy on the way home. He had had a lovely time. His pockets were full of sweets and chocolates, and he held his top in his hand. He even felt that he could forgive his family. He'd heap coals of fire on Robert's head by giving him a chocolate . . . He was almost asleep when the charabanc drew up at the post office. Everyone began to descend. He took a polite and distant farewell of the elderly lady and set off for his home. But he found that the elderly lady was coming with him.

'Where do you live?' she said.

'Oh,' said William vaguely, 'jus' somewhere along here.'

'I'm coming to see your father,' said the lady in a determined voice.

William was aghast.

'Oh – er – I wun't do that if I was you!' he said.

'I often find,' she said, 'that a drunkard does not realise what unhappiness he makes in his home. I often find that a few words of warning are taken to heart—'

'You'd better *not*,' said William desperately. 'He dun't mind *wot* he does! He'd throw knives at you or shoot you or cut your head off soon as not. He'll be jus' mad drunk when we get in. He went off to the public house jus' after breakfast. You'd better not come *near* our house . . . All I say *is*, you might jus' as well be *dead* as coming to our house.'

'But what about you?'

'Oh, I'm used to it,' said William valiantly. 'I don't mind. Please, you'd better not come,' he urged. 'I'm thinkin' of *you*—'

'I shan't feel that I've done my duty till I've at any rate tried to make him see his sin.'

They were in the street now in which William's family were living. William looked pale and desperate. Matters seemed to have gone beyond his control. Suddenly he had an idea. He would lead her past the house and on and on till one or other of them dropped from fatigue. She'd have to go home some time. She couldn't go on all night. He could say he'd forgotten where he lived. He began to dislike her intensely. Fussy ole thing! Believing everything everyone said to her! Interfering with other people's drunken fathers! He was creeping cautiously and silently past his house by the side of his unsuspecting companion, when a shrill cry reached him.

'William! Hi! William! Where have you been? Mother says come in at once!'

It was Ethel leaning out of an upstairs window. The sight of her pretty white-clad figure brought no pleasure to her brother's heart. He put out his tongue at her and sadly opened the garden gate.

'You'd better not come in,' he said faintly to his companion, in a last feeble attempt to avert the catastrophe which Fate seemed determined to bring upon him, 'he gets *vilent* about this time of day.'

With firm set lips his companion followed him.

'I must do my *duty*,' she said sternly.

*

53

Mr Brown looked up from the evening paper as his younger son entered. At first he merely noticed that his younger son looked unusually sheepish. Then he noticed that his son was followed by a tall, thin lady of prim appearance and uncertain age, wearing *pince-nez*. Mr Brown groaned inwardly. Had William killed her cat or merely broken one of her windows?

'Er – good evening,' he said.

'Good evening,' said the visitor. 'I have been spending the afternoon with your little boy.'

Mr Brown sent William a speaking glance. He didn't mind what caricatures William picked up outside the house, but he wished he'd keep them there. William refused to meet his father's glance. He sat on the edge of a chair looking rather pale, his cap in his hand, measuring with his eye the distance between the chair and the half-open door.

'Very kind of you,' murmured Mr Brown.

'He has told me something of the state of things in his home,' burst out the visitor. 'I saw at once that he was unhappy and half-starved.'

Mr Brown's jaw dropped. William very slowly and cautiously tiptoed to the door.

'He told me about you and his mother. I was sure – I am sure – that you don't realise what you are doing – what your – er – failing – means to this innocent child.'

Mr Brown raised a hand to his brow.

'Your conscience, you see,' said the visitor triumphantly, 'troubles you. Why should the memory of
childhood mean to that dear boy blows and curses and
unkindness – and just because you are a slave to your
baser appetites?'

Mr Brown removed his hand from his brow.

'You'll pardon my interrupting you,' he said feebly,
'but perhaps you would be good enough to give me some
slight inkling of what you are talking about.'

'Ah, you *know*,' she said fervently, 'in your soul – in
your conscience – you know! Why pretend to me? I have
had that dear child's company all afternoon and know
what he has suffered.' Here Mrs Brown entered and the
visitor turned to her. 'And you,' she went on, 'you must be
his mother. Can't you – won't you – give it up for the sake
of your child?' Her voice quivered with emotion.

'I think, my dear,' said Mr Brown, 'that you had better
send for a doctor. This lady is not well.'

'But who *is* she?' said Mrs Brown.

'I don't know,' said her husband; 'she's someone
William found.'

The someone William found flung out her arms.

'Won't you?' she cried eloquently. 'Can't you – for the

sake of your own happiness as well as his – give it up?'

They stared at her.

'Madam,' said Mr Brown despairingly, 'what do you wish us to give up?'

'*Drink*,' she answered dramatically.

Mr Brown sat down heavily.

'*Drink!*' he echoed.

Mrs Brown gave a little scream.

'*Drink!*' she said. 'But we're both teetotallers.'

It was the turn of the visitor to sit down heavily.

'Surely,' she said, 'that boy did not deceive me!'

'Madam,' said that boy's father bitterly, 'it is more than probable.'

When the visitor, protesting, apologising, expostulating, and still not quite convinced, had been escorted to the door and seen off the premises, Mr Brown turned grimly to his wife.

'Now,' he said, 'where is that boy?'

But a long and energetic search of house and garden failed to reveal any traces of him. It was not till an hour later that William, inspired more by pangs of hunger than by pangs of conscience, emerged from the boot cupboard in the kitchen and surrendered himself to justice.

CHAPTER 4

WILLIAM THE REFORMER

William's regular attendance at church on Sunday mornings did not betoken any deeply religious feelings on his part. It was rather the result of pressure from without, weekly applied and resisted by William with fresh indignation on each occasion. His church-going was a point on which his family insisted. It was not that they hoped that any real improvement of William would result from it. As a matter of fact, it generally seemed to have the opposite effect upon him. But it meant that those of his family who did not go to church had one morning at least in the sure knowledge that William's strident voice could not dispel their Sabbath peace and calm, nor could William, with his curious genius for such things, spring any awkward situation suddenly upon them, while those who went to church had the comfortable knowledge that William, cowed, and brushed, and washed, and encased in his hated best suit, and scowling at the vicar from the front pew, could do little harm beside the strange scuffling with his feet that he seemed able to produce without even moving them. Moreover, they 'knew where he was'. It was something to 'know where he was'.

This Sunday the usual preliminaries took place.

'I'm not going to church this morning,' Robert happened to say, carrying a deck-chair into the garden.

'An' I'm not, either,' said William, as he seized another chair. The would-be light finality of his tone did not deceive even himself.

'You must go, dear,' said his mother placidly. 'You know you always do.'

'Yes, but why me an' not him?' demanded William, pale with outrage. 'Why him not go an' me go?'

Robert calmly stated his position.

'If William's not going to church, I'm going, and if William's going to church, I'm not. All I want is *peace*.'

'I shun't make a noise if I stayed at home,' said William in a tone of righteous indignation at the idea. 'I'd jus' sit qui'tly readin'. I don't feel like bein' rough or anything like that. I'm not feelin' well at all,' he ended plaintively.

Mr Brown came downstairs, top hatted and gloved.

'What's the matter?' he said.

'William's too ill to go to church,' said Robert in an unfeeling tone of voice.

William raised his healthy, ruddy countenance.

'I'd like to go to church,' he explained to his father.

'I'm disappointed not to go. But I jus' don't feel well. I'm took ill sudden. I'd jus' like to go an' lie down qui'tly – out of doors,' he stipulated hastily. 'I feel 's if I went to church I might worry everybody with bein' so ill. I feel' – his Pegasean imagination soared aloft on daring wings – 'I feel 's if I might *die* if I went to church this mornin' feelin' 's ill as I do now.'

'If you're as bad as that,' Mr Brown said callously, as he brushed his coat, 'I suppose you might as well die in church as anywhere.'

This remark deprived William of the power of speech for some time.

'Well,' he said at last, darkly and bitterly, 'I only hope you won't be *too* sorry afterwards – when you think of what you've done. I only hope *that* – I only hope that when you think of what you've done *afterwards* – you won't be *too* sorry. When you—'

'Hurry up, dear,' said his mother patiently. 'Don't keep us all waiting.'

Sitting between Ethel and his mother in the front pew, William allowed his thoughts to wander at their own sweet will. He found the Litany very long and trying. Its monotony had been relieved only by a choirboy who occasionally brightened William's existence by putting out his tongue at him from behind the cover of his psalter. From that a contest in grimaces had arisen, begun furtively, but growing reckless in the heat of rivalry, till a choirman had intervened by digging the choirboy from behind, while Mrs Brown leant forward and frowned at William. William retired from the contest feeling distinctly exhilarated. He considered that most decidedly he had won. The choirboy could not have capped that last one of his. In a half-hearted way he began to listen to the sermon.

'We all owe our duty to others,' the clergyman was saying. 'We must all try to save others beside ourselves. Not one of us must rest content till we have recalled from evil ways at least one of those around us. How many there are going down the broad path of evil who want just the word to recall them to the path of virtue – just the word that the youngest here could say . . . ?'

William considered this view. He found it distinctly intriguing. He had been so frequently urged to reform himself that the appeal had lost its freshness. But to reform someone else. There was much more sense in that; he wouldn't mind doing that. His spirits rose. He'd rather like to try reforming someone else.

They stood up for the hymn. The choirboy was singing lustily. William caught his eye and began to imitate his more open-mouthed efforts. This led to a second contest in grimaces, checked for a second time when at its height by the choirman and Mrs Brown. William returned to his meditations. Yes, it would be a noble deed to reform someone else, much more interesting and less monotonous and possibly more successful than the reforming of himself hitherto solely enjoined upon him.

But who? That was the question.

After due consideration that afternoon in the apple tree (where William did most of his deep thinking) he came to the reluctant conclusion that he must exclude his family from the list of possible reformees. This was not because he did not think that his family were in need of reformation. It was not because he thought them beyond reformation, though he certainly was of that opinion. It was rather because he doubted whether any member of his family was sufficiently broad-minded to receive reformation at his hands.

There is a certain proverb about a prophet in his own country. His thoughts wandered over several masters at his school, whom he considered to be in crying need of reformation, but the same applied to them. When, finally, the tea-bell sounded forth its summons, he was still undecided on whom to apply his latent powers of reformation.

His family, who had not passed so peaceful a Sunday afternoon for weeks, looked at him in curiosity as he entered the dining-room.

'What have you been doing all afternoon, dear?' said his mother solicitously.

'Jus' thinkin',' said William coldly. Meditation on his family's need for reformation had made him realise afresh all he suffered at their hands.

'Not dead yet?' said Robert jocularly.

'No,' said William with a quelling glance, 'though anyone *might* be with what I've got to put up with. It's a good thing I'm *strong*.'

He then transferred his attention to a large piece of bread and butter and the conversation drifted away from him. Idly he listened to it.

'It's so funny,' Ethel, his grown-up sister, was saying, 'to come to a country place like this and take no part in the life. He's so mysterious. He took Beechwood over a month ago and hardly a soul's seen him. He never has anyone in and he never goes out.'

'Of course,' contributed Robert with the air of a man of the world, 'a country place like this is an ideal place for murderers or other criminals to hide in. That's notorious. Much safer than London.'

'And hardly anyone's seen him,' said Ethel.

'What does he look like?' said William excitedly.

'Don't talk with your mouth full,' said Ethel.

'Don't listen to their nonsense, dear,' said Mrs Brown.

But William was afire. Here was someone to be reformed at his very doors – no mere ordinary trivial wrong-doer, but a murderer, a criminal, the real thing. He was longing to begin. He could hardly wait till he had finished his bread and butter.

'May I go, Mother?' he said hastily, swallowing a quarter of a slice of bread as he spoke.

'You've had no cake, dear,' said his mother in surprise.

William gave a look of set purposeful determination.

'I don't want *cake* today,' he said in the voice of one who scornfully waves aside some trifle unworthy of him. With that he strode frowning from the room.

'I do hope he's not ill,' said Mrs Brown uneasily. 'He's been awfully quiet today.'

'He's given us the first peaceful Sunday we've had for years,' said Ethel.

'It's not over yet,' said Robert, in a voice of warning.

William was already on his way to Beechwood. In the road he found Ginger, his bosom friend on weekdays. On Sundays the two families, inspired solely by a selfish desire for peace, tried to keep them as far apart as possible.

'*Sunday!*' said Ginger, bitterly voicing unconsciously the grievance of the majority of his countrymen. 'There's nothing to *do*!'

'*I've* jolly well got something to do, *I* can tell you,' said William in a voice in which mystery and self-importance were mingled.

Ginger brightened.

'Lemme help!' he pleaded. 'Lemme help an' I'll give you half the next thing anyone gives me.'

'S'pose it's something you can't make a half of?' said William guardedly.

'Well, then, I'll let you have it in turn with me,' said Ginger generously.

'Fair turns?' said William.

'Rather!' said Ginger.

'All right, then,' said William. 'Come on!'

Ginger set off happily by his side.

'What you goin' to do, William?' he asked.

William sank his voice mysteriously.

'I'm going to *re*form,' (William put the accent on the first syllable), 'a murderer – make him give up murdering – same as what he said in church this mornin'.'

'Crikey!' said Ginger, impressed.

*

They crept in at the open gates of Beechwood.

'How're you goin' to begin?' said Ginger in a loud whisper.

'Dunno yet,' said William, who always trusted to the inspiration of the moment.

'S'pose – s'pose he murders us?' whispered Ginger.

'If he does,' said William grimly, still aggrieved by his family's general attitude to him, 'I know *some* folks that'll p'raps be *sorry* for *some* things!'

Then suddenly –

'He's there!' said William excitedly. 'Look! I can see him!'

They crept behind some bushes and watched. A man was digging in the middle of the lawn. He stood up to his neck in a large hole and was throwing up spadeful after spadeful of earth on to the edge. Occasionally he stopped to wipe his brow. He was a thin, youngish man.

'Diggin' graves for dead folks he's murdered,' explained William.

'Golly!' breathed Ginger, his eyes and mouth wide open. 'How're you goin' to stop him?'

'Get him in the hole,' said William, 'an' then – an' then – I dunno yet,' he ended uncertainly.

The man bent down for another spadeful.

'Come on!' said William.

They crept across the lawn and suddenly overturned the heap of fresh-dug earth that was on the edge of the hole upon its occupant, using feet and hands and head and body. It all happened in a second. The man, up to his neck in the sudden avalanche of damp garden soil, looked up at them, sputtering anger and earth.

'I say! I say, you know,' he said. 'Look here!'

William leant over the edge of the hole.

'You jus' gotter *stop* it,' he said fiercely. 'D'you see? You jus' gotter *stop* it!'

The young man gazed at him in amazement. He made no effort to arise. He lay back on his earthen couch.

'You've jolly well winded me, you young devil!' he said, still ejecting earth from his mouth as he spoke. 'Stop what?'

'*You* know,' said William mysteriously, bending still farther over the edge of the hole. 'You jolly well *know*, doesn't he, Ginger? How'd you like someone to do it to you – murderin' you an' buryin' you in back gardens? Jus' think of that! Jus' think of how you'd like *other* folk doin' it to you, 'fore you start doin' it to other folks.'

'I'll jolly well murder you, once I get out of here,' said the man. 'I'll murder you and bury you ten times over. Don't worry about that.'

'You oughter reform an' start again on the – what was

THEY CREPT ACROSS THE LAWN AND SUDDENLY
OVERTURNED THE HEAP OF FRESH-DUG EARTH OVER THE
EDGE OF THE HOLE UPON ITS OCCUPANT.

it? – the path of virt – virt something – now I've told you
like what he said – with jus' a *word*. Well, I've said the
word, an' you oughter *re*form an'—'

'Just you wait, my son,' said the young man grimly,
beginning to unearth himself.

But Ginger had made a discovery.

'Look, William,' he said. 'Look at this!'

'This' was a tin, containing curious earth-covered coins, at the edge of the hole.

'He's a thief, too,' said William indignantly. 'Takin' folks' money as well as buryin' them. He's goin' right down the broad evil path like what he said. Well, he oughter stop. I've said it. I've said the word like what he said, an' he oughter *re*form an' come back to the path of virt— what he said.'

The young man was fast unearthing himself. He looked a curious sight.

'Just you wait,' he said again, as he began to climb out of the hole. 'Murder won't be in it.'

Instinctively and throwing the zeal of the reformer to the winds, William and Ginger took to their heels and fled – across the lawn, down the drive, down the road – with fleetness of foot gained in many a flight from irate farmers and landowners. Ginger still hugged to his breast the tin of coins. The earthen young man followed, leaving a trail of soil as he ran.

'Here!' he shouted. 'Bring back that tin! Here! *Thieves!*'

They threw him off at the first turning, and made for William's house. They fled panting up the drive.

'Look out!' said William breathlessly. 'There's Father!'

Mr Brown, putting on his hat in the hall for a quiet

evening stroll, turned to see his son and his son's friend walking slowly and demurely up the drive. The son's friend held an old tin clasped to his breast. Both were red and breathless in spite of their slow and demure progress. Mr Brown looked at his son with a suspicion born of experience.

'Where have you been?' he said.

'Jus' for a walk,' said William meekly and with wide-eyed, appealing innocence.

The two proceeded towards the stairs.

'Where are you going now?' said Mr Brown, still more suspiciously.

'Jus' up to my room, Father,' said William.

Mr Brown fastened his stern gaze upon the tin.

'What have you got there?' he demanded.

'Jus' some ole things we've found,' floated in William's dulcet tones from halfway upstairs.

'Crumbs!' said William upstairs. 'I thought he was going to nab us.'

'My sainted aunt!' said William's father downstairs, 'That boy's up to *something* again!'

William's father, however, soon forgot William. It was a perfect evening. Sabbath calm reigned supreme over the countryside. The trees were just beginning to turn from green to gold. The birdsong rang through the still evening air. As Mr Brown walked along, a sense of peace and well-being descended upon him. He completely forgot William. Then, suddenly, he turned a bend in the road and saw a curious figure – so curious that Mr Brown pinched himself to make sure he was awake. Sabbath calm ceased to reign supreme over the countryside and Mr Brown's sense of peace deserted him. The figure was that of a hatless, wild-eyed young man, covered to the neck in soil, and bearing traces of it upon his face.

'I say,' he began abruptly, 'are you a resident of these parts?'

'Yes,' admitted Mr Brown, debating in his mind on the safest method of dealing with an escaped lunatic.

'I've been robbed. Some most valuable coins. Simply robbed in broad daylight.'

'You'd better go to the police about it,' said Mr Brown soothingly. 'Come with me. I'll show you the way.'

He thought the police station the best receptacle for the strange wanderer.

'I've taken Beechwood, you know,' went on the excited young man, 'and I'm doing some excavating there on my own. I belong to the Archæological Society. I've found traces of Roman occupation here. I've had some experts down and there's no doubt that there was a Roman villa on the site of Beechwood. I found some most valuable coins this afternoon and I've been robbed of them. They're irreplaceable!'

'Who stole them?' said Mr Brown. He was rather bored by the whole proceeding. He was anxious to deposit the strange young man in the police station and continue his walk.

'Mere boys,' said the young man. 'Mere boys. They pushed earth in on me and shouted some gibberish and made off with the coins. Probably some rival collector heard of the thing and sent them.'

'Probably,' agreed Mr Brown without interest. 'Well, here's the station. I'll say goodnight and good luck.'

He touched his hat and was on the point of proceeding with his walk, but the young man was pathetically anxious to confide the whole tale.

'I've really no clue,' he said sorrowfully. 'The coins were in an old tin – simply an old tin. Well, I suppose I'd better go in. Goodnight.'

Mr Brown was standing motionless. He seemed to have lost all desire to proceed with his walk. His smile had faded from his face. He was seeing a sudden vision of two small boys, red-faced and breathless, but wearing looks of innocence that blazoned guilt far and wide, creeping cautiously upstairs. One of the boys had held an old tin in his hand – simply an old tin. He turned to the young man. The young man had already reached the door of the police station.

'Here!' shouted Mr Brown. 'One minute!'

The man returned to him.

'You said boys,' said Mr Brown slowly. 'What sort of boys? Could you describe them?'

'One was freckled,' said the young man. 'He called the other one Ginger.'

Mr Brown swallowed.

'I think,' he said, 'that I can help you – if you'll come home with me.'

'Have you got a clue?' said the young man excitedly.

'I think,' said Mr Brown, 'that I have.'

The young man, dropping garden soil with every movement upon Mrs Brown's drawing-room carpet, clasped his tin box to his breast – William, frowning and injured, stood before an accusing family circle and defended himself.

'Well, how was I to *know*? I found him diggin' graves for the folks he'd murdered. I was trying to *re*form him – like what he said in church. How was I to *know* that he wasn't diggin' graves for the folks he'd murdered? I wanted to *re*form someone same as he said. He *said* he was a mur-

derer too – he as near as near murdered Ginger an' me –
how was I to *know*?'

The young man interrupted, with a quick movement
and another shower of garden soil at which Mrs Brown
shut her eyes and breathed an inward prayer.

'Look here!' he said. 'It was all a misunderstanding. I

WILLIAM DEFENDED HIMSELF. 'WELL, HOW WAS I TO KNOW?
I FOUND HIM DIGGIN' GRAVES FOR THE FOLKS HE'D
MURDERED.'

say, suppose you come to tea with me tomorrow and we bury the hatchet instead of the murdered – eh? I say, I'd better go and change, hadn't I?'

'I'll see you down the road,' said Mr Brown.

The young man went off, happily clasping his tin and scattering earth thickly around him.

The rest of the family turned to William.

'Well, you've done it *now*!' said Ethel.

'I *said* Sunday wasn't over!' said Robert.

'The carpet is simply *ruined*!' moaned Mrs Brown.

'Well – how was I to *know*?' said William desperately.

'It's ever so long after your bedtime, William,' said Mrs Brown with a sigh. 'He's simply *trodden* the stuff in besides putting it there.'

'I advise you to go to bed before Father comes back,' said Robert with a superior elder-brother air.

William inwardly agreed. There was something to be said for being in bed and asleep when his father came home. Explanations, put off to the following day, are apt to lose the keenness of their edge. He turned to the door.

'Nothing I do ever seems to come out right,' he said gloomily. 'How was I to *know* – diggin' away like that?'

'I daresay you didn't mean anything, dear,' said Mrs Brown, 'but it was only new last January.'

William reached the bottom of the staircase, then had

a sudden thought and returned.

'Anyway,' he said, putting his head round the drawing-room door, 'if you hadn't made me go to church when I was feelin' so ill, I wun't have known anything about *re*forming folks.'

'William,' said Mrs Brown wearily, 'do go to bed.'

William complied, but again only reached the foot of the staircase. Here another thought struck him, and he returned.

'Anyway,' he said, putting his head round the door again, 'I bet *you* wun't have gone right up to a murderer, diggin' a grave for the folks he'd murdered, an' I bet if he *had* been a real murderer an' I'd been dead *an'* buried by now, *you'd* be feelin' a bit—'

'William,' said Mrs Brown, 'are you going to bed?'

William again retired. This time he got halfway upstairs. Then a third thought struck him and again he descended.

'Anyway,' he said, and his family groaned as the familiar untidy shock of hair and frowning freckled face once more appeared. 'Didn't Ethel say that he never had folks in, an' isn't he having me in to tea tomorrow, so I bet you can't say I haven't *re*formed him.'

'*William!*' said Mrs Brown. 'Are – you – going – to – bed?'

William *was*. He had heard the click of the gate at the end of the drive.

When William's father entered the house three minutes later, William was in bed and asleep.

CHAPTER 5

NOT MUCH

William walked down the village street singing lustily. His strident, unmelodious young voice rang out harshly. His face was purple with vocal effort.

> *Dare to be a Daniel,*
> *Dare to stand alo – o – o – one,*
> *Dare to have a purpose true – ue – ue,*
> *Dare to make it know – ow – ow – own.*

Becoming tired of that subject and not knowing the next verse, he abruptly changed his tune –

I'm longing for the dear ole home agai – ai – ai – ain,
That cottage in the little winding la – a – a – ne,
I can see the roses climbing, I can hear the sweet bells
  chiming,
And I'm longing for the dear ole home agai – ai – ai – ain.

Inhabitants of the street along which William was passing

hastily shut their front windows or fled from their front rooms or uttered loud objurgations of William according to their characters. William passed along, singing and unmoved. A parrot, who had refused all invitations to converse since its purchase, suddenly raised its voice with William's in piercing screams. The quiet street had become a nightmare uproar of inharmonious sound. A man threw a boot at William from an upstairs window. It hit a hen in a neighbour's garden. The hen added its voice to William's and the parrot's. William passed along, singing and unmoved –

I've a girl in Navara,
I've a girl in Sahara,
I've got a few sweet girlies who – o – o – o I've promised
  to – o – o be true – ue – ue – ue to – o – o – o.

He turned off the main street. The hideous sound died gradually away in the distance and quiet reigned once more in that vicinity. Windows were opened, people returned to their front rooms, the parrot relapsed into his customary silence.

William went on singing towards his home. At the gate of his garden he changed his song for a toneless penetrating whistle. He whistled his way blithely up the drive. His father flung up a window fiercely.

'Stop that noise!' he called.

William proceeded on his way.

'Stop – that – noise!'

William stopped.

'What noise?' he said.

'That – that foul noise you were making just now.'

'Whistlin'? I din't know you meant whistlin' when you said noise,' William went on, drawing near the window. 'I din't know you was talking to me at all jus' at first. I thought—' William was obviously anxious to carry on a friendly conversation with a fellow being. His father hastily slammed the window and returned to his armchair.

William opened his mouth as for a burst of song. Then he seemed suddenly to change his mind and pursed his lips as if for a whistle. Then, after a breathless moment of silence, he unpursed them and humming untunefully under his breath he entered by the side door.

The hall was empty. Through the open kitchen door he could see his mother and Ethel, his grown-up sister, cutting sandwiches at one table and the cook and housemaid at another. He went into the kitchen.

'Who're you makin' sandwiches for?' he demanded.

His mother surveyed him sadly.

'I do wish you could keep clean for more than two minutes together, William,' she said.

William smoothed back an obstreperous mop of hair with a grimy hand.

'Yes,' he agreed mechanically, 'but who're you makin' sandwiches for?'

Ethel paused with a butter-laden knife in mid-air.

'Don't for Heaven's sake tell him,' she said, 'and let's hope and pray that he'll keep out of the way till it's over. It'll be enough trouble without him hanging round.'

William ejected the tip of his tongue in her direction behind his mother's back.

'Yes – but – who're – you – makin' – sandwiches – for?' he said slowly and emphatically, with an air of patience tried beyond endurance.

'I think he'd be rather a help than otherwise, you know,' said his mother, carefully arranging pieces of tongue on a slice of bread and butter.

Ethel merely shrugged her shoulders.

'I s'pose,' said William with heavy sarcasm, 'you're makin' them jus' for fun?'

'Clever!' said Ethel, cutting off the crusts of a sandwich.

William, whose appetite was a never-failing quality, fell upon the crusts and began to eat them.

'Don't spoil your lunch, dear,' murmured Mrs Brown.

'No,' promised William, 'but – all – I – want – to – know – is – who're – you – makin' – sandwiches – for?'

'Oh, do say something and stop him saying that awful sentence,' groaned Ethel.

'Well, dear,' began his mother persuasively, 'would you like a little party this afternoon?'

'People coming to tea?' asked William guardedly.

'Yes, dear, you'd be such a help – and—'

William interrupted.

'I'll eat up all they leave afterwards for you,' he said obligingly; 'but I think I won't come this time.'

'Thank Heaven!' murmured Ethel.

'I'm not much good at parties,' said William with perfect truth and with a perfunctory grimace at his sister.

'But wouldn't you like to help to hand things round, darling?' asked Mrs Brown.

'No, thanks, but I'll eat up all they've left for you afterwards.'

'How kind!' said Ethel.

William, goaded at last to verbal retaliation, turned on her.

'If you say much more to me,' he said darkly, 'I'll – I'll – I'll not help *you* at any of your parties.'

He then echoed her derisive laughter in a piercing tenor.

'William, darling,' sighed Mrs Brown, 'do go and wash your face.'

William crammed a handful of crusts into his mouth, put the cushion from the armchair on to the top of the cat, and went out into the hall. Here he burst suddenly into a flood of raucous sound –

> *Oh, who will o'er the downs with me?*
> *Oh, who will with me ri – i – i – i – ide?*

Mr Brown opened the library door.

'Will – you – stop – that – confounded – noise?' he demanded emphatically.

'I'm sorry,' said William amicably. 'I forgot you din't like musick.'

After lunch William sallied forth once more into the world. He was feeling slightly bored. Ginger and Douglas and Henry, his three sworn allies, were all away on their holidays. William did not consider holidays unmixed blessings. Anyway, he considered that there ought to be a law that everyone should go on their holidays at the same time. He walked again down the village street. He did not sing this time. Instead he threw stones at the telegraph poles. He stood at one telegraph pole and tried to hit the one across the road. Every pole that was hit was to William a magnificent tiger, falling lifeless, shot by William through the heart. The parrot, catching sight of him again, gave an excited scream. This put William off his aim. He screamed back at the parrot, missed the telegraph pole and hit a King Charles spaniel in a garden. He then dropped the rest of his stones and fled from the indignant owner of the dog. She pursued him down the street. 'You cruel boy – I'll tell your father – a poor dumb animal—' She gave up the chase at the end of the road, and William went on his way whistling, his hands in his pockets. At a bend in the road he stood suddenly silent. A group of children were walking along in front of him. They had evidently just come out of the station. At their head walked a tall, thin man. The children – boys and girls – were about William's age. They were clean and tidy, but badly dressed, and with pale cockney faces. William hurried along the road. A little girl turned round.

' 'Ullo,' she said with a friendly grin, 'did yer nearly git left be'ind? Wot's yer nime?'

William liked the almost incredible frizziness of her over-crimped hair. He liked the dirty feather in her hat and the violent blue of her dress. He liked her white stockings and yellow boots. He thought her altogether and entirely charming. He liked the way she talked. He found her whole personality intriguing. His grim freckled features relaxed into an ingratiating smile.

'William,' he replied. 'Wot's yours?'

'Heglantine,' she said. 'Noice nime, ain't it? Me sister's called 'Oratia. Loverly, comin' on the trine, weren't it?'

It was evident that she took him for one of her party. William grasped at the opportunity of continuing the acquaintance. 'Um,' he said non-committally.

'Din't see yer on the trine. Such a crawd, weren't there? Some from St Luke's an' some from St Mary's. Oi dunno 'aft of 'em, an' don't think much o' some of 'em by their looks. Oi were jus' lookin' aht fer someone ter pal up wif.'

William's heart swelled with delight at this implied superiority. A boy in front turned round. He was pale and undersized and wore a loud check cap that would have fitted a grown man.

''Ullo, Freckles!' he said to William.

William glared at him fiercely.

'You jus' mind wot you say to me,' he began darkly.

Eglantine quickly interposed.

'Nah then, Elbert 'Olmes,' she said sharply, tossing her tight curls and feathered hat. 'None of your fice 'ere! You mind wot yer syes ter me an' my frens.'

The boy grinned and dropped behind with them.

'Wot we goin' ter do, anywyes,' he said in a mollifying

tone of friendship. 'Not much ter do in the country, is there? No pishers, no nuffin'.'

'There's gimes,' said William, deliberately adopting the accent of his new friends. He decided to adopt it permanently. He considered it infinitely more interesting than that used by his own circle.

'Gimes!' said the boy in the check cap with infinite scorn. 'Runnin' rices an' suchlike. An' lookin' at cows an' pickin' flowers. Thanks! *Not much!*'

William stored up this expression for future use.

'Well, yer needn't of come, Elbert 'Olmes,' said Eglantine sharply, 'if yer din't of wanted to.'

'They said,' said Elbert grimly, 'as 'ow there'd be a tea, an' oi'm not one ter miss a tea – a proper tea wif cike an' all – *not much*!'

William was watching the large check cap with fascinated eyes.

'Where'd you get that cap?' he said at last.

'Dunno,' said the boy. He took it off and looked at William's.

'Loike ter swop?'

William nodded. The boy whipped off the cap without a word and handed it to William, taking William's school cap in return. William, with a sigh of bliss, put it on. It enveloped his whole head and forehead, the large peak standing out over his nose. He pulled it firmly down. It was the cap of his dreams – the cap of a brigand chief.

'We hare smart, ain't we?' said Eglantine with a high-pitched laugh.

William felt blissfully happy walking along beside her.

'Wot does yer farver do?' demanded Elbert of William suddenly.

'Wot does yours?' replied William guardedly.

''E goes rahnd wiv a barrer sellin' things,' said Elbert.

'Moine sweeps chimeneys,' said Eglantine shrilly, ''e gets that black.'

They both turned to William.

'Wot does yours do?'

William bowed his head in shame. He could not bear to confess that his father neither sold things nor swept chimneys, but merely caught a train to London and his office every morning.

'Ain't got no father,' he said doggedly.

'You're a horphin, then,' said Eglantine, with an air of wide knowledge of the world.

'Umph,' grunted William.

At this point the tall, thin man in front stopped and collected his flock around him. He wore a harassed and anxious expression.

'Now,' he said, 'are we all here? One – two – three –

WILLIAM FELT BLISSFULLY HAPPY WALKING ALONG
BESIDE HER.

four,' he counted to himself, wagging a thin forefinger round the group as he spoke.

'Plears, sir, William's a horphin,' said Eglantine excitedly.

'Yes, yes,' said the tall man. 'Let me see – I seem to make you one too many, but no matter – William an orphan? How sad! Poor little fellow! Come along. We're going to play in the woods first, children, and then go to a kind friend's to tea. The Vicar rang her up this morning and she very kindly offered to give you tea. Very kind! Very kind! Yes, yes. This way, I think.'

Again the little procession moved on its way.

'Softie!' commented Eglantine scornfully. ''E's one of the swanks, 'e is! 'E's a friend of the Vicar's, 'cause the Vicar couldn't come. Ain't got no patience wiv 'em myself. Whoi carn't they talk like other folks?'

William redoubled his efforts to acquire his friend's intonation.

'Yes, whoi-oi'd loike ter know,' he said aggressively, pulling his large and loud tweed cap yet farther over his eyes. The tall, thin man at the head of the procession stopped again.

'I'll just go into this house, children,' he said, 'and ask the way to the woods.'

He went up the pathway and knocked at the door. The

group of children clustered round the gate and watched him. The door was opened by a housemaid. The thin man disappeared inside. The door was shut.

'Are we going to hang round *him* all the time?' asked William discontentedly. 'Won't be any fun – *not much*,' he added proudly, after a slight pause.

'Well, 'e knows the wye an' we don't,' said Elbert.

'I do,' said William. 'You come with me – quick – afore he comes out.'

They followed William silently round the back of the house and across a field. From the other end of the field they had a glimpse of the tall man coming out of the house, taking off his hat with a polite bow, then standing at the gate and looking round in bewildered amazement. Then they disappeared over a stile into another road. Here a small person at the rear of the procession set up a plaintive cry.

'Oh – oo – oo,' she sobbed, 'I'm tahred of the country. Oo – oo – oo, I want to gow 'owm.'

Eglantine came to the rescue.

'If you don't shut up makin' that noise, Christine 'Awkins,' she said, 'a cow or sumphin'll eat you up. Yer never knows in the country.'

The sound ceased as by magic. William led his friends along the road. At a pair of iron gates leading past a lodge into a winding drive, Eglantine stopped.

'I'm tahred of walkin' along this 'ere road,' she announced. 'Let's go in here.'

Even William was aghast.

'It's someone's garden,' he explained.

'Fought yer could go anywhere yer loiked in the country,' said Eglantine aggrievedly. 'That's wot they said, anyway. They said yer could go anywheres yer loiked in the country. Dunno whoi we cime,' she ended wearily.

The shrill wail rose again from the back of the crowd.

'Oo – oo – oo – oo, I'm tahred of the country. I want to gow 'owm.'

Eglantine entered the gate determinedly.

'Come orn!' she said.

'They'll turn us out,' said William.

Eglantine squared her thin shoulders.

'Let 'em jes' troi turnin' *me* aht,' she said.

'*Not much*,' murmured William proudly.

They passed with no opposition up the first part of the drive. Then Eglantine saw a hedge with a gate in it and marshalled her party through that. Within they saw a lawn, some gardens, and a fountain.

'Looks orl roight,' commented Eglantine loftily.

A young man rose languidly from a hammock in the trees.

'I beg your pardon?' he said politely.

'Grarnted,' said Eglantine, not to be outdone in politeness.

'Can I do anything for you?' said the young man.

'We're St Luke's and St Mary's,' explained Eglantine importantly.

'I see,' said the young man. 'You, I presume are a St Mary, and he of the horsey headgear is a St Luke.'

''Im?' said Eglantine, pointing at William, ''e's a horphin.'

The young man adjusted a monocle.

'Really,' he said, 'how intensely interesting!'

'We've come into the country fer a 'oliday,' went on Eglantine, 'an' we jes' cime in 'ere ter see wot it was loike in 'ere.'

'How extremely kind of you!' said the young man, 'I hope you like it.'

Eglantine surveyed the scene distantly.

'Wiv a band an' some swings an' a hice cream cart, it'd be orl roight,' she admitted.

The young man sighed.

'I suppose so,' he said.

Most of the children were already making the best of their opportunities. Some were chasing butterflies, some picking flowers, some had taken off shoes and stockings and were paddling in the ornamental pond. The young man watched them rather despondently.

'If I'd known that you were coming,' he said, 'I'd have procured something in the way of a band and ice-cream cart.'

Eglantine again was not to be outdone in politeness. She stood, a curious picture, in her blue dress, white stockings, yellow boots, with her over-frizzed hair standing out around her sharp little face beneath her feathered hat, and nodded slightly.

'Hits of no consequnce,' she said graciously.

She had the situation entirely in hand. Even William, born leader as he was, was overshadowed by her, and was content that it should be so. Just as two small boys had climbed the pedestal in the middle of the ornamental pond and were endeavouring to stop up the fountain, a butler came down the path with an expression of horror on his face. The young man waved him away.

'It's all right, Thomson,' he said.

'Yes, sir,' said the man, 'but her ladyship has arrived, sir. Her ladyship has had her boxes sent upstairs. I thought I'd better warn you, sir.'

The young man groaned.

'Is there time for me to be summoned to town?' he asked.

'I'm afraid not,' replied the butler. 'She's coming to find you now, sir. Here she is, sir.'

A large woman bore down upon them. She wore a large cloak and a large hat, and several Pomeranians trotted at her heels.

The young man rose to receive her.

'Here you are, Bertram,' she said. 'You didn't invite me, but I've come.'

'How awfully good of you,' said the young man dispiritedly.

The lady put up her lorgnettes and surveyed the children.

'Who – are – these – ragamuffins?' she said slowly and distinctly.

'Oh, just a nice little party of mine,' said the young man pleasantly. 'St Luke's and St Mary's. You'll get awfully fond of them. They're very lovable.'

The lady's face became stony.

'Are you aware,' she said, 'that they're trampling on the flowers and splashing in the pond and sitting on the sundial?'

'Oh, yes,' he smiled. 'Just jolly childish pranks, you know.'

'And that one in the awful tweed cap—'

'He's an orphan,' said the young man. 'I'm going to give you the room next to his. He's got quite a jolly voice.

I heard him humming to himself a moment ago.'

At this point four things happened.

One – William, who had wandered over the flower beds, was suddenly impelled by the general brightness of the day to give vent to his feelings by a burst of song –

One more river, an' that's the river of Jor – or – or – ordan,
One more river, there's one more river to cross . . .

He yelled the words happily in his strident young voice.

Two – The small pessimist again lifted up her voice in a wail. 'Oo – oo – oo – oo. I'm tahred of the country I want to gow 'owm. Oo – oo – oo.'

Three – Eglantine, who had surveyed the visitor in outraged silence for a few moments, at last burst forth. She set her thin hands on her thin hips and began.

'An' oo're you ter talk abaht ragamuffins? Queen of Hengland, are yer? An' wot abaht yer own 'at? A-hinsultin' of hother people in hother people's gardings.'

Four – The five Poms, excited by the uproar, burst into simultaneous yapping.

Above the horrible sounds of William's song, the pessimist's wails, Eglantine's recriminations, the Poms' yapping, the lady screamed to her nephew.

WILLIAM YELLED THE WORDS IN HIS STRIDENT YOUNG
VOICE.

'I'm going straight home, Bertram. When you have a Christian house to invite me to, perhaps you'll let me know.'

'Yes, Aunt,' he screamed back. 'Shall I see you to your car?'

He left them for a few minutes and returned, mopping his brow, in time to rescue three boys from an early death from drowning in the pond. William and a few other daring spirits were balancing themselves at a dizzy height on the top of the wall. The young man was beginning to look pale, when once more the butler appeared.

'There's a gentleman at the front door, sir,' he said respectfully, 'who seems in a great state, sir, and he says that he's lost some slum children—'

The young man's face brightened.

'Ah,' he said, 'tell him I've found some, and ask him to come and see whether they happen to be his. They've done me a very good turn, but I shouldn't mind being relieved of them now.'

' 'E was one of the swanks an' no mistake,' said Eglantine to William. 'Oi'd no patience wiv 'im an' 'is wye of talkin'. Oi can plye the toff as well as anyone when oi loikes – oi did wiv 'im, din't oi? But oi despises 'em.'

William was looking anxiously down the road where

the tall man was taking them.

'Where we goin'?' he said distrustfully.

'To the kind lady's who invited us to tea,' said the tall man, overhearing him.

William walked along in silence. Eglantine began to expatiate again.

'Look at all them 'ouses,' she said, with a contemptuous glance at the houses between which they were passing. 'Wot they want wiv such big 'ouses? Swank! That's all it is. Swank! Livin' in big 'ouses an' talkin' so soft. Oi've no patience wiv 'em. Oi wouldn't be one of 'em – not fer nuffin'.'

But William was growing more and more uneasy.

'What we're goin' along here for?' he muttered truculently.

The tall man turned in at a gate. William moistened his lips.

'He's making a *mistake*,' he murmured, pulling his check cap still farther over his eyes.

At the door stood Mrs Brown and Ethel. Their glance fell first on Eglantine.

'What a dreadful child,' whispered Mrs Brown.

Next it fell on all that could be seen of Eglantine's companion.

'What an appalling cap!' whispered Ethel.

Then they advanced to welcome them.

'Here we are,' said the tall man, with a note of relief in his voice. 'Here we are . . . we've had a delightful time – er – quite a delightful time – er – on the whole – er – just a little misunderstanding at one point – a – temporary separation, but all's well that ends well. It's too kind of you. This is – er – Eglantine, and – er – this little boy is an orphan, poor little chap!'

Mrs Brown laid her hand tenderly on the tweed cap. 'Poor little boy,' she began. 'Poor little—' then she met the eyes beneath the tweed cap. '*William!*' she said sharply. 'Take off that horrible cap and go and wash your face.'

William, clean and brushed and frowning, sat and glared across the table at his late friends. He felt himself disgraced for ever. He was a pariah, outside the pale, one of the 'swanks' who lived in big houses and talked soft. His mother's and Ethel's intonation and accent seemed at that moment a public humiliation to him. He did not dare to meet Eglantine's eyes. Fiercely he munched a currant bun. Into his unoccupied hand stole a small grimy one.

'Never moind,' whispered Eglantine, 'yer carn't 'elp it.'

And William whispered gratefully, '*Not much.*'

CHAPTER 6

WILLIAM AND THE WHITE CAT

William had before now met the strange species of male who succumbed to the charms of his elder sister. William never could think what people saw in Ethel. Red hair and blue eyes and a silly little voice . . . Some people (thought William) might call her pretty – but, crumbs, what a temper! – making a fuss if his dog Jumble chewed up any of her old things, or if he jus' borrowed her bicycle, or if his pet rats got loose in her room.

She didn't even like interesting things like pistols and rabbits and insects. Girls were bad enough when they were at school, thought William, but they were heaps worse when they grew up.

The female sex was an entire mystery to William. Except in the case of his mother, he could see no reason for their existence. Yet he grudgingly admitted to himself that Ethel's admirers had not been useless to him. There was Mr French, who had given him his first couple of white rats, there was Mr Drew, who had showered rare postage stamps upon him, there was Mr Loughton, who had nervously pressed sixpence into his hand whenever they met . . .

But Mr Romford was different. He had a strange idea that William had no influence with his elder sister. This happened to be true, but that made it none the less annoying to William. He thought it only right that any young man who was interested in Ethel should ensure his (William's) sympathy by practical means. Mr Romford treated him as if he did not exist. William resented this very much.

'Wot's he *come* for?' he said, indignantly. 'He doesn't take no interest in Jumble, nor the rats, nor the toolshed, nor the bridge wot I'm making over the stream, nor *me*. Wot's he come for?' he demanded of his assembled family.

They all replied to him.

Ethel said coldly: 'Don't talk about things that aren't your business.'

His mother said: 'William, I wish something could be done about your hair. It never looks tidy!'

His father said: 'That reminds me, William, you'd better go and weed your garden. It's in a disgraceful state.'

William went slowly to the door.

'Mr Romford's going to give me a Persian cat for a Christmas present,' Ethel went on to her mother.

William stopped.

'Wot about Jumble?' he said, indignantly. 'Wot about Jumble with an ole cat about the place? Wot about my rats? How d'you think they'll like an ole cat about the place? My rats 've got as much right to live's an ole cat, you'd think, wun't you? My rats an' poor ole Jumble came here first, I *think* – I *think* they did, considering that the ole cat hasn't come yet. You'd think that Jumble an' the poor ole rats deserved a *bit* of peace . . . '

'Go and give your hair a good brushing, William,' said his mother.

'Take every one of those weeds up. You can't have touched it for weeks,' said his father.

'You aren't the only person in the world who can keep animals,' said Ethel.

'A lot of int'rest you take in animals, don't you? – in *real* animals.' William exploded bitterly. 'A lot of int'rest you take in my insecks an' rats an' things, don't you? I mus' say you take a lot of int'rest in them,' he went on in heavy sarcasm.

'Cats! Who'd call cats an animal? They aren't int'restin', are they? Who ever found cats int'restin'? They don't follow you like dogs, do they? They haven't int'restin' habits like insecks – oh, I mus' say they're very int'restin'!'

He saw Ethel and his mother gathering breath to speak. His father had retired behind a paper.

He hastily went out, shutting the door firmly behind him.

'*Cats!*' he remarked, contemptuously, to the empty hall.

William was walking slowly along the road, with his hands in his pockets, whistling. He felt at peace with all the world. He had a half-crown in his pocket. It would soon be Christmas. He was going to have a bicycle for Christmas. Ethel had insisted on his having a bicycle for Christmas, not for love of William, but because William's secret experiments with her bicycle had such dire results.

'He'll only smash it up, if he has one, dear,' his mother had said.

'Well, he'll only smash up mine, if he doesn't,' Ethel had replied.

So William was going to have a bicycle and a mouth organ and pocket-compass in addition, of course, to the strange things always sent as presents by distant aunts and uncles. Those did not count – pencil-boxes, and story-books about curious, exemplary boys, and boxes of crayons and pens and things. They didn't count.

Anyway, a bicycle was a bicycle. He wanted to be able to take a bicycle right to pieces and put it together again. He'd never been able to have a really good try at Ethel's. She made such a fuss. He was thinking about this, with a faint smile on his face, when he observed a man coming along with a covered basket in his hands. It was Mr Romford. William looked at him coldly. He had no hopes of a Christmas present from Mr Romford but Mr Romford stopped.

'Are you going home, William?' he asked.

'Yes,' said William ungraciously.

'Would you mind taking this to your sister? It's a present I am giving her for Christmas. Don't open the lid. It's a very valuable white cat.'

William took it. Something was moving about inside.

'It's in a highly nervous state,' went on the donor; 'I shouldn't look at it if I were you.'

'All right,' said William, coldly.

William walked on down the road. His smile had gone. He no longer thought about Christmas. He swung the basket carelessly as he walked. An infuriated scratching and snarling came from inside. William swung it still more carelessly.

'I'm not a cat-carrier,' he muttered, indignantly. 'Makin' me into a cat-carrier for him!'

He sighted Ginger, his ever faithful friend and ally, in the distance, and hailed him with a piercing whistle. Ginger came to him.

'What d'you think's in here?' queried William.

'Dunno!'

'An ole cat! An' whose d'you think it is?'

'Dunno!'

'Well, a man's givin' it to my sister. An' how much d'you think he's givin' me for takin' it?'

'Dunno!'

'*Nothin'!*' said William, bitterly. 'Nothin'. Makin' a cat-carrier of me for nothin'.'

'Listen to it!' said Ginger, enraptured.

'It's been carryin' on something dreadful ever since I got it,' said William. 'It's a beautiful, nice quiet cat, isn't it? It'll be nice for Jumble an' those poor ole rats when this sort of wild thing gets loose, won't it? It'll be nice for them, then.'

Sarcasm was a new weapon of William's, and as yet his use of it was heavy.

'Let's have a look at it,' said Ginger.

'Oh, yes,' said William. 'It's all right for you. You aren't going to have looks at it all the res' of your life. You aren't going to have your life an' the lives of your dog an' rats made a misery by it for the rest of your life. I don't feel inclined to waste time lookin' at it. Listenin' to its carryin' on's enough for me *jus'* at present. You've not been made a cat-carrier for nothing. You don't feel like I do about it.'

'Let me jus' peep, William.'

'All right, if you take any int'rest in it. I don't. I should think there's some law about givin' wil' animals for presents. There oughter be. Human life oughter be sacreder than wot it seems to be to him. All right. Look at it. Don't blame me if it leaves its mark on you for life. It's a nice, quiet-tempered sort of cat. Oh, yes! Very!' He laughed sarcastically.

Ginger cautiously opened the basket top a fraction of an inch.

A small, white paw shot out. Ginger closed it hastily and sucked his hand with an expression of agony on his face.

'Golly!' he ejaculated.

'There!' said William, triumphantly. 'Didn't I tell you? It'll prob'ly give you blood poisoning. All I hope is, if you die of it, he'll get hung. He oughter be – sendin' wild cats without tamin' them first.'

Ginger assumed a heroic expression.

'It wasn't much of a scratch. Let's have another look.'

He opened the lid of the basket again. Both William

and Ginger disclaimed responsibility for what followed. William said he wasn't touching it, and Ginger said that he only opened it a bit and he didn't know that the creature was mad – not really mad – not right off its head like that. Anyway, a white ball of fury hurled itself out of the basket, dealt William a long scratch across his cheek, nearly tore off Ginger's ear, and disappeared over the nearest wall.

'Well,' said William, coldly. 'What you going to do now?'

'*Me?*' said Ginger.

'Yes. Jus' tell me how you're going to replace a valu'ble cat wot you've just let loose. Jus' tell me wot I'm goin' to do. Am I going home to say I've got a valu'ble cat, in a highly nervous state, and then them find there's nothing in the basket but jus' air? This is all I get for being his cat-carrier! Well, you let it loose, an' you've got to *re*place it. That's sense, isn't it? I was jus' quietly carryin' a valu'ble cat, in a highly nervous state, down the road, an' you come along an' let it loose. Well, wot you goin' to do?'

'Well, wot can I do?' said Ginger, helplessly. 'I din't know the thing was a cat lunatick, did I? It oughter be in a cat asylum. You never told me you was carryin' a wild cat or a mad cat. You jus' said a cat. You—'

But the white ball of fury had appeared again, flying

over the wall and down the road at full speed. William grasped his empty basket, and started after it.

'Come on!' he shouted, as he ran. 'Come on! Catch it! Catch it!'

They raced down the road after the flying white ball – first the cat, then William, then Ginger – through a garden, leaving a cursing gardener in their rear – in and out of a house, leaving its irate owner ringing up the police – first the cat, then William, then Ginger, breathless and afire with the chase.

Along a wall, the cat on the top and William and Ginger at the foot.

They nearly got her then. She fell into a rain-tub in a private garden at the foot of the wall, but scrambled out and fled again, dripping and grimy . . . through a muddy ditch . . . the ball of fury was now not white, but a dingy grey . . . and suddenly right into a tabby cat with a broken ear, who was washing its face by the roadside. There was a whirl of claws and flying fur . . .

'Get it now!' yelled William. 'Get it while they're fighting.'

Ginger seized the basket and effected the capture neatly, but not without a dozen or so more scratches. They fastened up the basket and resumed their journey.

'Well, you can't say I din't do that, can you?' said

THE WHITE CAT RAN SUDDENLY INTO A TABBY CAT WITH A
BROKEN EAR. THERE WAS A WHIRL OF FURY. 'GET IT NOW!'
YELLED WILLIAM. 'GET IT WHILE THEY'RE FIGHTING!'

Ginger, vaingloriously. 'You can't say I din't do that pretty
neatly! You can't say you helped much there. I bet if *you'd*
all these scratches there'd be some sort of a fuss!'

'Yes, and who let it loose? That's all I'm asking. Who
let it loose? . . . Oh, come on! Let's get it home. I'm about
sick of it. I'm about sick of being his cat-carrier!'

They walked along in silence for a bit.

'Seems a bit quieter, doesn't it?' said Ginger.

'Speck it knows now it's no use makin' a fuss. Speck it

din't quite know before wot sort of cat-catchers we was.'

'Let's have another look at it, William!'

'Oh, yes, an' go lettin' it loose all over the place again. Oh, yes, do!'

'It's quiet now. It'll not mind me lookin'. I want to see if it's got very dirty.'

William weakened.

'I'll have a look at it this time,' he said, 'then p'raps it won't get loose all over the place!'

Cautiously he opened the basket lid. Over his face came a look of horror. It faded, leaving it grim and scornful.

'Oh, yes, you did it,' he said, with heavy sarcasm. 'You did it pretty neatly, as you said you did. Oh, yes, I din't help much. Oh, yes, you caught it.'

He opened the basket wider. A friendly tabby, with a broken ear, regarded them and gave a tentative purr.

'Oh, yes, you caught it all right, but you caught the *wrong* one!'

Ginger looked at it, aghast, speechless. Then he pulled himself together.

'Well, we'll have to pretend that it's the one.'

'Oh, yes,' said William. 'She'll believe it's a valu'ble white cat, in a highly nervous state, won't she? Oh, yes, she's quite likely to believe that!'

They sat down by the roadside and stared at each other hopelessly. The tabby showed no signs of wishing to leave them, though, in their despair, they had left the basket open.

'We – might do something to make it nervous,' suggested Ginger, feebly.

He began to make strange noises of obviously hostile and insulting intent to the cat. The cat began to purr. William watched with cold scorn.

'Oh, yes, and then do somethin' to make it valu'ble, an' then do somethin' to make it white!'

They were both strangely silent at this last suggestion. The hopelessness of their countenances seemed to clear.

'It mightn't stay on, of course,' said William, 'but it might make it look all right for a bit.'

'Where can we get some?' asked Ginger, cryptically.

'P'raps old Lawkins has some,' said William. 'You can pay for it.'

They carefully replaced the tabby cat in the basket and went towards the village shop.

William entered and stated his needs.

'White paint?' said the shopman. 'I think so. I think so. For iron work?'

'Well,' admitted William, 'it's really for fur – I mean—'

he corrected himself hastily, 'for somethin' – for somethin' a bit softer than iron.'

'For wood?' suggested the old man.

'I 'speck that'd do,' said William, 'and a brush too, please.'

They retired to a deserted field to perform the delicate task.

William took the brush in one hand and put down the paint-pot on the grass by his feet. Then he took out the cat.

'Now, *I'm* going to do this,' he explained, 'because I want it done prop'ly. I don't want this cat let loose all over the place.'

He held the cat in one hand and drew a bold line of white paint down its back. The next moment he was sucking a deep, red scratch on either hand, and a white-flecked tabby cat was disappearing in the distance.

'You did that all right, din't you?' said Ginger, not without satisfaction.

William rose wearily, picking up the empty basket. He was too disheartened even to save what was left of the paint.

'Oh, let's leave it and go home,' said Ginger.

'Oh, yes, that's all right,' burst out William. 'It's all right for *you*. You've not to go home and say you've lost a valu'ble white cat, in a highly nervous state, wot someone was giving to Ethel.'

'Well, what can I do?' snapped Ginger.

'You can perduce some sort of a cat,' said William firmly. 'That's all I say. You let the first one loose all over the place, and you can perduce another. That's all I say. I'm not going home without some sort of a cat. I don't mind about it bein' valu'ble, or white, or nervous; but I must go home with some sort of a cat. All I ask you is to perduce some sort of a cat.'

'I wish you'd stop saying that,' said Ginger, irritably.

'Well, perduce one an' I will,' said William, imperturbably.

'There ought to be lots of cats about,' said Ginger. 'Let's go to the road again.'

They went down the village street. Only one cat was to be seen. William and Ginger approached it cautiously.

'Pretty pussy!' said William, hoarsely.

'Puss, puss, puss!!' said Ginger, in honeyed accents.

'Pretty pussy! Pretty pussy! An' I feel more like murderin' it,' said William.

The cat sidled up to them.

William picked it up, stroking it affectionately with an expression of intense hatred on his face.

'Open the basket, Ginger, quickly.'

'Mother!' came a shrill voice to his rear. 'Boys is stealin' our cat!'

William dropped the cat and fled down the road, followed by a broomstick, flung after him by the cat's owner, and a stone thrown by the child. The extent to which William's spirit had been broken by his troubles was shown by the fact that he endured these outrages without retaliation.

When it was safe to relax his speed, he turned to Ginger.

'I'll try one more cat,' he said, 'and that's all. I've done with cats after that.'

They found one more cat. It responded to William's oily flattering. It deigned to be taken up in his arms and stroked.

It was not till it was almost lowered into the basket that it showed the falseness of its friendliness. Its wildness then surpassed even the wildness of the first occupant of the fateful basket.

'Well, I've done with cats,' said William solemnly, withdrawing his hand from his mouth and watching the furry, flying creature in the distance. 'I've done with cats. If they was to come in crowds now, *askin'* to be put in the basket, I wun't touch them. I've *done* with cats. I'll feel sick whenever I see a cat for the rest of my life.'

A boy came down the road, his pockets bulging with something that moved.

'What's that?' said William, without interest or spirit.

The boy took out a small furry animal.

'Ferrit. Me Dad catches rabbits with 'um! You've gotter be careful 'ow you 'olds 'em.'

'Will you sell it?' asked William sadly, taking out his half-crown.

'It's not a cat,' said Ginger, wearily.

But William had not lost his optimism.

'Some folks don't know much about animals,' he said, hopefully. 'They might think it was a cat!'

William's father and mother and sister were in the morning-room when he entered with his basket. He held it out to Ethel.

'There's your cat,' he said.

'From Mr Romford?'

'Yes,' said William, gloomily.

She opened the lid a fraction, then shut it in silence. She looked mystified.

'It isn't a cat!'

William's face was expressionless.

'All I can say is wot he told me,' he said in a monotonous voice. 'He said it was a valu'ble white cat, in a highly nervous state.'

'*This?*'

'It may have got a bit mixed up on the way, but that's what he said. He said that it was a valu'ble white cat, in a highly nervous state.'

'You needn't keep on saying that,' said Ethel, irritably.

'It's wot he said,' said William, doggedly. 'He said distinctly that it was a valu'ble white cat, in a—'

'Be quiet, William!'

William's father came across the room and held the lid open, peering in. Suddenly he withdrew his finger with a yell of pain and rushed from the room, uttering muffled curses.

'Do you mean to say, William,' said Mrs Brown, 'that Mr Romford sent Ethel that – whatever it is?'

'All I can say is wot he told me,' said William. 'He said it was a valu'ble—'

'Mother, if William says that once more I shall go mad.'

William came across to it curiously.

'Let's have a look at it,' he said. 'Oo – ow – *ow*! It's bit me!'

It was out of the basket suddenly and across the room. Ethel gave a piercing scream. It met Jumble in the hall, and a mad chase ensued – scampering down the hall – round the drawing-room – the crashing of a small table and all its ornaments – the ferocious growling of Jumble – then silence.

'I can't stand much more of this,' said Mrs Brown. 'I don't know what's the matter, or what the animal is, or whether it's killed Jumble or Jumble's killed it – but how

'BE QUIET, WILLIAM,' SAID WILLIAM'S SISTER. WILLIAM'S FATHER LIFTED THE LID AND PEERED IN. SUDDENLY HE WITHDREW HIS FINGER WITH A YELL OF PAIN.

any man could send . . . for a Christmas present, too . . . William your finger's bleeding, and it's covered with dirt. You'd better go and wash it.'

'Yes, Mother,' said William meekly.

Then he saw a man coming up the drive carrying the dirty, bedraggled white cat.

'Look!' he said in an awestruck voice. 'That's him.'

'It's Mr Romford,' said Ethel.

She went out into the hall. The conversation was distinctly audible.

'How d'you do, Miss Brown? I'm afraid there's been some little accident. I've—'

'Thank you very much,' said Ethel, coldly. 'But we don't want any more *cats* here.'

'I'm afraid there's been a mis—'

'The kindest thing to think, Mr Romford,' said Ethel, 'is that you hadn't the least idea what you were doing.'

'There's been a mis—'

'My father and my poor little brother have been very badly injured. These things often prove fatal.'

'There's been a mis—'

'My mother is terribly upset by it. You must excuse me if—'

'I can explain, Miss Brown—'

'I dare say you can. You must excuse me. Goodbye.'

She shut the door and returned to the morning-room.

'Go and wash you hands, William,' said Mrs Brown.

William was watching Mr Romford's crestfallen departure. His indignation returned.

'Makin' me his cat-carrier!' he muttered.

'William, will you go?'

'An' how much do you think he gave me for bringing it?'

'I've no idea, and if once the dirt gets right into a bite like that—'

'*Nothin*',' said William, dramatically, as he turned to the door.

CHAPTER 7

WILLIAM'S SECRET SOCIETY

William considered that the microbe world was treating him unfairly. Mild chickenpox would be, on the whole, a welcome break in the monotony of life. It would mean delicacies such as jelly and cream and chicken. It would mean respite from the pressing claims of education.

It would afford an excuse for disinclination to work for months afterwards. William was an expert in the tired look and deep sigh that, for many months after an illness, would touch his mother's heart and make her tell him to put his books away and go out for a walk. No one could rival William in extracting the last ounce of profit from the slight indisposition.

And now Henry, Douglas and Ginger, William's bosom friends and companions in crime, had all succumbed to chickenpox, and chickenpox had passed William by, leaving him aggrieved and lonely. William himself spared no effort. He breathed in heavily the atmosphere of Ginger's Latin Grammar, on which Ginger had been lately engaged, as soon as he heard that Ginger had fallen a victim. It was no use. William caught nothing.

So William was left alone, bereft of his faithful friends, gloomily picturing their existence as one glorified holiday. But his troubles did not end there. Mr Cremer, William's peaceful and long-suffering form master, became ill, and the next morning his place was taken by Mr French.

William's attitude to his schoolmasters was, as a rule, one of pitying forbearance, but he was, on the whole, quite kindly disposed to them. He indulged their whims, he smiled at their jokes, he endured their sarcasm; but he refused to concentrate his mental powers on x's and y's and dates like 1815 in the few precious hours that were at his disposal in the evening. Instead of doing homework, he preferred to play at Red Indians or Pirates, or to hunt for rats and rabbits with Jumble, his mongrel dog.

Until the coming of Mr French, William's relations with his schoolmasters had been fairly amicable. Mr Cremer was a pacifist. He wanted peace at any price. He frankly avoided conflict with William. If he saw William quietly engaged in drawing beetles during his lesson, he did not expostulate. He thanked Heaven for it. He was not a proud man.

But Mr French definitely disliked William. He kept him in till unreasonable hours in the evening. Upon William's making a quiet and unostentatious exit by way of the window when his back was turned, he followed William to his home, appeared suddenly when William was sitting down to a delayed but welcome meal, and led him ignominiously back.

When William and his special friends, according to their time-honoured custom, had bought a large pork pie, to be passed surreptitiously round for a bite each, in order to beguile the tedium of a geometry lesson, Mr French descended upon William as he was in the act of making the first bite, and condemned him to consume the mountainous whole before the assembled form. It was not that the pork pie was really too much for William's digestive capacity. It was that even William felt the procedure to be lacking in dignity. Moreover, there was a stormy meeting afterwards of shareholders in the pie, who demanded their money back . . .

But it was when William had spent the whole of afternoon school laboriously writing the first chapter of what was to be an epoch-making story, and Mr French had seized upon it, read it aloud to the form, and then burnt it publicly and disdainfully, that William felt it was time that something happened to Mr French. He was proud of that story; he thought it sounded a jolly good yarn, even when read by Mr French, who didn't seem to know how to pronounce half the words.

'The pleecemen rushed upon the outlor as he stood there so proud an' manly.

'"Ho, ho!" he cried. "Come on, varlets, an' I'll jolly well show you."

'With one sweep of his gorry blade three pleecemen's heads roled of into a heep. He shot another through the brane, another fell strangled, an' another, wot had a week hart, fell down dead at the horrible site. Only one was left.

'The outlor gave a snarling laugh through his clenshed teeth.

'"Come on varlets," he said, waving his gorry blade in one hand an' his gun in the other, an' holding a dagger in his clenshed teeth.

'But the pleeceman slank of.

'"Coward!" taunted the outlor through clenshed teeth.'

William felt strongly that it was a very good story. He'd have to write the whole thing out again now. It was certainly time something happened to Mr French. He went home planning vengeance.

He walked home slowly, his brow drawn into a stern frown, not leaping in and out of the ditch, or hurling missiles at passing friends or enemies, as was his usual custom. His thoughts were so entirely taken up with schemes of vengeance that he walked past the turning that led to his home and found himself in a road through which he did not often pass.

Two boys stood outside the gate of a house. They were boys whom William's mother would have designated as 'common'. William, whose tastes were lamentably low, looked at them with interest. He felt suddenly lonely and eager for the society of his kind. The opportunity of an introduction soon occurred. The larger of the two boys looked up to find William's scowling gaze fixed upon him.

'Ullo, Freckles!' he called, accompanying the insult with a grimace of obviously hostile intent.

William, forgetting all thoughts of Mr French in the exhilaration of the moment, advanced threateningly.

'You jus' say that again,' he said.

The red-haired boy obligingly said it again, and William closed with him. They rolled across the road and into the ditch and out of it again. William pulled the red-haired boy's nose and the red-haired boy rubbed William's head in the dust. It was quite a friendly fight – merely an excuse for the display of physical energy.

The second boy sat on the fence and watched. Every now and then he spat in the dust with a certain conscious pride. At last, friendly relations having been established by the bout, William and the red-haired boy sat up in the dust and looked at each other.

'What's your name?' demanded William.

'Sam. Wot's yourn?'

'William. D'you go to school?'

The red-haired boy looked scornful.

'School? Me? No much! I'm workin', I am. I works there, I does.' He cocked his thumb in the direction of the house. ''E ain't much catch, though, 'e ain't. Stingy ole blighter – never so much as says 'take an apple or two', or 'take a bunch of grapes or two' – not 'e – an' me the gardener's boy.'

He relapsed into pensive gloom at this recital of his woes.

'So don't you never get none?' said William sympathetically.

'*Don'* I?' said Sam with a wink. 'Wot d'yer think? That's all I asks yer. Wot d'yer think? But it 'ud be friendlier in 'im ter ask me ter 'ave one or two. Not,' he admitted, 'as it makes much difference. But 'e's a stingy bloke – allus 'as been. 'E's one of these 'ere schoolteachers. Kinder disagreeable in 'is manner.'

'What's his name?' said William, with sudden interest.

'Ole Frenchy we calls 'im,' said Sam. 'An' don' 'e think 'e's clever? Not 'arf. Ho my!'

Into William's inscrutable countenance had come a gleam of light. For a moment his thoughts worked silently and daringly.

'Would you like,' he said at last, 'to b'long to a secret serciety?'

Sam put his cap on one side and chewed a blade of grass ruminatively.

'Dunno,' he said. 'Never tried. Leastways, not as I can call to mind.'

'Well,' said William, persuasively, 'you can try now. I want to start one an' you can b'long. I want you to b'long 'cause you're his gardener's boy an' can *do* things – 'cause he's awful mean an' made me eat all the ole pie an' burnt my tale an' said lots of things an' I want to make a secret serciety for payin' him out.'

Sam seemed to grasp the situation.

'Orl right,' he said, 'an' wot do I get fer it?'

This slightly nonplussed William.

'Oh,' he said vaguely, 'it's a serciety – you jus' b'long – you – er – well, you jus' *b'long*.'

Sam was considering the idea.

'Let's 'ave 'im,' he said, pointing at the boy who was still sitting on the fence and spitting proudly at intervals. ' 'E's errand boy at the grocer's, he is, an' 'e's offen round 'ere. 'E's called Halbert, 'e is.'

Albert was approached, and expressed himself willing to join.

'I don't mind b'longing,' he said, with a sigh of deep feeling. 'I wouldn't mind *murderin'* of 'im sometimes, when 'e tells me to get out of 'is garding scornful like. I would 'a' murdered 'im long ago if it 'adn't been for my poor ole mother.'

Even William was startled.

'You needn't *murder* him,' he said, hastily. 'He's only gotter be paid out.'

The Secret Society of Vengeance met for the first time the next afternoon, in an old barn on the hillside.

Albert had brought a friend of the name of Leopold to swell their numbers. Leopold wore a tweed cap, many sizes too large for him, pulled down over his eyes. It gave him a daredevil air. He announced, in a husky voice, that he 'din' care nuffin' fer no one, so there!'

William looked round at his small band with a proud heart. Though he had not forgotten the aims of his secret society, it was the fact of its existence that really thrilled him.

'Now we've gotter take a sacred an' solemn oath,' he said, 'an' sign it in our blood, an' get a secret password an' a secret sign an' a secret langwidge.'

Leopold created a diversion by announcing, briefly and

gruffly, that no one was going to sign nothing in his blood. When threatened with ejection by William, and taunted with cowardice by Sam, he flung himself upon them in dramatic fury. They moved hastily aside in opposite directions, and his outstretched fist came heavily in contact with a nail in the barn door. As an adequate supply of blood seemed to be promptly assured, he lost his anger and became unbearably conceited, parading his bleeding fist and commenting on some people he knew who would have made a fuss and no mistake over a little thing like that. He didn't mind a little thing like that – he'd – well, anyway, hurry up with that oath, or it would be drying up.

William had found in his pocket a grimy piece of paper and the stump of a pencil, and was writing with a set, purposeful expression.

'Now listen,' he said at last. 'This is wot I've wrote: "We, wot our names are sined in blood under this riting, take an oath to revenge to the deth any member of this serciety wot is treated unfair. This is a Secret Serciety. The punishment for anyone wot does not revenge anyone else, or wot tells about the Serciety, is not to be spoke to or played with by any of the other people in the Serciety for ever till deth." '

The signatures were the next difficulty. Leopold signed his with a scornful pride that was beginning to make him unpopular. William, feeling that his reputation as founder of the society was at stake, took out a battered penknife, made a slight incision with a dramatic gesture, and signed his name beneath Leopold's. Albert said he wasn't going to cut his finger, 'cause he was afraid of bleedin' to death, an' then he wouldn't be able to support his poor ole mother when he was a man. He'd got some red paint at home and he was going to fetch that. He wouldn't take a minute. He repeated that he wouldn't mind cuttin' off his head if it wasn't for his poor ole mother. Leopold's airs were becoming insufferable. He ejaculated, 'Ho, yuss!' at intervals during Albert's speech, but the rest of the society seem to be agreed to ignore him for the present. Sam, with an exaggerated expression of agony, manfully endured, had been coaxing a two days' old scratch, and had just completed his signature when Albert returned with the red paint.

When the document was complete, William folded it up and put it in his pocket.

'Now,' he said, assuming a businesslike attitude, 'we've gotter think of a secret password.'

Leopold darkly suggested ' 'ell', but it was felt that, though sinister, it was too indefinite. Albert, after deep thought, brought forward the proposal: 'Hengland hexpects'. This was felt to be, on the whole, too lofty, and finally Sam's suggestion of 'Down wiv tyrants!' was accepted.

William (proposed and seconded by himself) was elected President, and the others (also on his proposal and seconding) were elected secretaries.

A whistle of penetrating and inharmonious tone was originated by William as a secret sign of danger, at which the whole society was to rally. Further, a member of the society, on meeting another member, was to cross the thumb and first finger and to utter darkly the words 'Outlaw – Brother!' Finally, each member raised his right hand, uttered slowly and solemnly the fatal words 'Down wiv tyrants – till death!' and the meeting dispersed.

Mr French became thoughtful. The morning after he kept William in he found (with painful consequences) a hornet in his boot. The evening after he had showered on William his choicest sarcasms he found the back tyre of his bicycle punctured. After another conflict with William, he found various indispensable things missing from his bag when he arrived at school, though he could have sworn he had put them in. He found them later in the greenhouse.

On another occasion he found that a little soot had been put in his hat and had reposed on his head as he paid a call and (all unconscious of his appearance) had tried to charm his headmaster's daughter. It was incredible, but— He pondered deeply over the matter and always came to the same conclusion. It was incredible, but— He tried ignoring William, and the curious, inexplicable annoyances ceased. It was certainly incredible, but— He left it at that.

The aims of the society widened. When Mr Beal, the squire of the villlage, chased William in person out of his orchard, with the help of dogs, sticks, and stones, he found the next morning in his orchard, in full view of the road, a scarecrow bearing a curious resemblance to himself and wearing a suit of his old clothes . . .

When the Rev. Cuthbert Pugh called William 'a nasty, dirty little boy, and, I am sure, a great trial to his dear mother', he discovered, the next morning, horrid little gargoyle-like faces outlined in white paint on all his trees – most unpleasant – and conspicuous – and unclerical.

It was altogether a successful secret society. It achieved its aims. It gave William back his self-respect, which Mr French had considerably impaired. The secretaries, Sam, Albert and Leopold, seemed to take delight in avenging the insults heaped by an unsympathetic world on their President. It was pure joy to William to meet any of them in the streets or lanes, cross his finger and thumb and utter darkly the words 'Outlaw – Brother!'

So far all was well . . .

*

Then Ginger, Henry and Douglas, recovered from chicken-pox, came back to school. The peaceful and inoffensive Mr Cremer returned to his own form room, and Mr French retired to his own fifth form. Mr French was not sorry to go. He went with one last speculative look at William, and with the final thought that it was incredible, but—

Life held once more games and walks and daring adventures with Ginger, Henry and Douglas. William lost his sense of grievance. He realised from his friends' accounts of their illness that he had not missed much. Gradually the once thrilling thought of his secret society ceased to thrill him. At first he took delight in uttering the mysterious password when he was with Ginger, Henry or Douglas, but he became bored with it himself, even before it got on their nerves, and they took active physical measures to get it off their nerves.

'All right,' agreed William, picking himself out of the ditch and removing the dead leaves from his hair and mouth. 'I won't say it again, but I jolly well won't tell you *why* I uster say it. It's a deadly secret an' I guess you can't guess wot it means.'

'Yes, an' I guess we jolly well don't want to,' returned Ginger.

It was the next week that William called a final meeting

of the secret society to announce its dissolution. As the members appeared, he realised how intensely he disliked them, Leopold especially. He hated Leopold now. He hated his large cap and little eyes and projecting teeth. He looked at him coldly and critically as he made his speech.

'The Serciety's gotter stop now, 'cause I've gotter lot of other things to do an' we're making a bridge over the stream in the field, an' I've not got time for secret sercieties, an' I don't want revenging any more 'cause he's gone now, an' so we'll stop it.'

'Wot about "till deth"?' said Leopold, hoarsely.

'Things is changed since then,' said William.

'Ho, yuss!' said Leopold, scathingly.

William's dislike of Leopold increased.

'Anyway, I made it,' he said aggressively, 'so I can stop it.'

'Orl right,' said Sam. 'You can pay us off an' stop it.'

'Pay you off?' repeated William, aghast.

'Yuss,' agreed Albert. 'You pay us off an' we'll stop it.'

'Ho, yuss!' said Leopold.

'I've not got anything to pay you off with,' said William, desperately. 'You don't be *paid* for bein' in a secret serciety. I told you you didn't. You jus' *b'long.*'

'Well,' said Sam, as if astounded by the depravity of human nature, 'an' us workin' for you—'

'Riskin' our lives for you,' put in Leopold, pathetically.

'To be treated like this 'ere,' ended Albert, sadly.

'But – wot d'you want?' said the President, wildly. 'I've not *got* any money left this week, an' next week's an' the week's after's goin' to pay for an ole clock bein' mended wot I was jus' lookin' at an' I put it back all right, 'cept how was I to know there was too many wheels in it? An' I tell you you don't be *paid* for bein' in a secret serciety – no one is – they jus' – they jus' *b'long* . . . I keep *tellin'* you . . . you don't *understand*.'

'Wot about "till deth"?' put in Leopold again in his sepulchral tones.

'Orl right,' said Sam, 'we'll jus' go an' tell ole Frenchy an' Mr Beal an' Mr Pugh an' your father that we did all those things, but you put us up to them an' made us do 'em.' He gazed at William dispassionately. 'I'm sorry for *you*. *You'll* catch it.'

William's freckled countenance was full of horror and amazement. He passed a grimy hand through his already wild hair.

'But – but it's not *right*. You don't understand. It's a serciety. You did the things 'cause you *b'longed*. You can't go an' tell of them afterwards. You – you don't understand.'

'We won't tell of them if you'll pay us off,' said Sam.

'Wot about "till deth"?' said Leopold triumphantly, with an air of bringing forward an irrefutable argument.

William took refuge in sarcasm.

'I *b'lieve* I've told you,' he said, with a passable imitation of Mr French's manner, 'that I've no money. I shall be very glad to *make* some money for you out of nothing if you'll show me how. Oh, yes! If you can show someone wot's not got any money how to *make* some money out of nothing, I'll make some for you – as much as you like. Oh, yes! I hope,' he ended, remembering one of Mr French's favourite phrases, 'that I make myself quite clear.'

They gazed at him in unwilling admiration of his eloquence. Sam brought them back to the matter in hand.

'It needn't be money,' he said. 'All we say is we oughter get something for all the trouble an' danger we've took for you. Something to eat would do – something nice an' big.'

'Yes, an' how am I to *get* it?' demanded William, indignantly. 'D'you want me to *starve*? D'you think my folks would look on an' watch me starve to death givin' my food to you – jus' 'cause you went an' put an ole scarecrow in someone's garden? D'you think that's a good reason for one person to starve to death, 'cause another person put a scarecrow in another person's garden?'

They were aware that in rhetoric William soared far beyond them.

'Well, we'll go home with you,' said Sam, ignoring the argument.

'Either you jus' give us something nice an' big to eat or we'll tell your father.'

William, though rather pale, laughed scornfully.

'Yes, you jus' come home with me,' he said. 'I guess you've not seen our dog, have you? Nearly as big as a horse. I guess there won't be much of you left when our dog sees you. Huh!'

With what was meant to be a sinister laugh he turned on his heel and strolled off. With sinking heart he saw that they were accompanying him, Leopold and his projecting teeth walking by his side, Sam and Albert behind. With a slight swagger and humming airily to himself, but with apprehension at his heart, William slowly wended his homeward way.

At the gate stood Jumble, his dog, small and friendly and rapturously glad to see them all. Jumble was no snob. Having assured William of his lifelong devotion and ecstatic joy at seeing him again, he went on to extend a tempestuous welcome to Sam, Albert and Leopold. William looked at him with affectionate sorrow. Though he adored Jumble, he thought he'd ask for a bloodhound for his next birthday present – a really savage one that would recognise his enemies at a glance. He walked, still with his careless swagger, but with his heart sinking lower at every step, round to the side door. Sam, Albert and Leopold still accompanied him.

'Now,' whispered Sam, 'you go and get us something real slap-up to eat, or we'll tell your father what you made us do.'

William entered the side door and shut it firmly.

He went first to the kitchen. Cook was lifting a large pie out of the oven. His gloomy expression lifted.

'Wot's that for, Cook?' he enquired, politely.

'For some people as is coming to supper tonight, an' none of your business, Master William.'

There was no love lost between William and Cook. William wandered casually over to the larder door and opened it gently. Cook wheeled sharply round.

'Please come away from that door and go out of my kitchen, Master William. Your tea's laid in the dining-room.'

William uttered his famous scornful laugh.

'Huh! If I wanted anything to eat, I wun't come *here* for it. I wun't care to eat anything out of *this* larder. My goodness! I'd sooner starve than eat stuff out of *this* larder, if I make myself quite clear.'

Cheered by these crushing remarks, but still apprehensive of what the next few hours might bring him, he went into the dining-room. His spirits rose still further at the sight of a lavish meal, but dropped as he noticed the presence of his mother and grown-up sister, Ethel. He would have preferred a clear field for his operations.

He uttered the mumbling sound with which he generally greeted his family.

'You're rather late, dear,' said his mother. 'Are your hands clean?'

William replied by the same non-committal grunt, pushed back his untidy hair with his hands, then hastily sat down, keeping his hands beneath the tablecloth till public interest in their colour should have waned. Through the window he could plainly see the forms of Sam, Albert and Leopold standing outside, and his apprehension increased.

'Mother,' he said faintly, 'it feels kind of stuffy in here. May I take my tea out into the garden? I think I could eat it better there.'

Mrs Brown looked at him anxiously.

'Do you feel ill, darling?'

'Kind of,' said William. 'I feel kind of as if I'd like to have tea out of doors. I could eat quite a big tea, but only out of doors. It's that kind of a feeling. Sort of as if I felt faint and not hungry indoors, but would be all right an' wantin' a big tea in the garden.'

'Fiddlesticks!' remarked Ethel, coldly.

'If you feel like that, darling,' said Mrs Brown, 'I think you'd better lie down. I'll bring you up a nice little tea on a tray.'

William perceived that Sam was grimacing at him through the window and pointing meaningly to the table.

'It's not that sort of a feeling at all,' said William. 'It's quite a different sort. I'd like jus' cake – lots of cake – in the garden. I'd feel all right then, if I could jus' take a lot of cake to eat outside.'

'William!' said Mrs Brown, who had moved over to the window. 'Who are those boys in the garden?'

William moistened his lips.

'Which boys?' he said, innocently, but with an expression of grim despair.

'There! By the hedge. They're pulling faces at you.'

'Oh, *those*!' said William, as if seeing them for the first time. 'Do you mean *those*?'

'Who are they, William?'

'Those boys?' said William slowly, to gain time. 'Jus' frens of mine. That's all. Jus' frens of mine that was interested in gardens an' wanted to see—'

'But they're horrid, common, rough boys.'

William gave a hollow laugh.

'Oh, no,' he said. 'They're not really. They only *look*

like horrid, common, rough boys. They're *dressed* like horrid, common, rough boys. They—'

'Don't talk nonsense, William. Go and tell them to go away at once. Have you finished your tea?'

William glared bitterly at the people who seemed bent on bringing about his doom.

'Oh, yes,' he said. 'I've had all the tea I feel like having in here. I don't know what'll happen to me later on,' he went on pathetically, 'with not having been able to have my tea the way I felt like—'

'Go and send those boys away at once, William, and never bring them here again.'

William, whose opinion of life in general was, at this moment, unprintable, went slowly into the garden.

'You've gotter go away,' he said in a hoarse whisper. '*She* says so.'

'Orl right. We'll go an' tell your father—'

'No,' said William, 'you wait by the gate an' I'll bring you something soon an' – my goodness – it'll be a long time before I go in for any more secret sercieties!'

They went furtively down the garden drive, and William returned to the house.

The guests were arriving. He caught sight of the Rev. Cuthbert Pugh and Mr Beal as they were ushered into the drawing-room. He hovered disconsolately round the

THROUGH THE WINDOW WILLIAM COULD PLAINLY SEE THE
MENACING FACES OF SAM, ALBERT AND LEOPOLD.

'WHO ARE THOSE BOYS?' ASKED HIS MOTHER.
'THOSE BOYS?' SAID WILLIAM SLOWLY, TO GAIN TIME.
'JUS' FRENS OF MINE.'

kitchen. Cook was securely in possession. She watched his every movement suspiciously. The position was desperate. Something must be done.

At any moment the story of his crimes might be laid before his father. As cook opened and shut the larder door, he caught sight of a large pie, with brown, crisp-looking pastry, upon the top shelf. That surely would pay off the blackmailing ex-secretaries of the Secret Society of Vengeance.

Quickly William formed his plans. To go to the larder by the kitchen door was impossible. But, somehow or other, he must get that pie. He went out of the front door and crept round the house to the larder window. It was unlatched. He opened it quietly and climbed in. Holding his breath in suspense, his fierce and scowling gaze fixed upon the door that led to the kitchen, he took the pie and silently climbed out again. There was exultation in his heart. The end was in sight. But he reckoned without Cæsar.

Cæsar was a boarhound belonging to Mr Beal, who accompanied his master on all his social calls, and waited outside the front door for him. On this occasion he seemed to be labouring under the delusion that William was kindly bringing some refreshment for him to beguile his long evening.

He advanced to meet William with tail wagging, and nose eagerly sniffing the delirious perfume of veal and ham pie. His whole being expressed anticipation and gratitude.

William said 'Down!' in a fierce whisper, and held his precious pie high above his head. Cæsar pranced along by his side, his eyes uplifted towards the heavenly smell. William had planned to creep through a shrubbery to the side gate, but it is difficult to creep through a shrubbery holding a heavy pie above one's head in close company with an enormous dog, whose energies are wholly concentrated on obtaining possession of the pie. William managed the situation for some time. He said 'Down!' often, and fiercely, and straggled on bravely, dragging the pie aloft through laurel and holly bushes. But Cæsar felt at last that he had been trifled with long enough.

He rose on two legs, placed his paws on William's shoulders, impelled him gently to the ground, and plunged his nose into his delicious supper. William sat up, nibbed a bruised elbow and looked around. Cæsar's appetite and capacity were unlimited. Half the pie had disappeared already, and the rest was fast disappearing.

'Crumbs!' said William, remembering the title of a book he had read lately. 'Talk about *Dogged by Fate*!'

With that thought came the thought of the hero of the book, Dick the Dauntless. *He'd* have thought nothing of a thing like that. *He'd* have thought nothing of taking on Sam and Albert and Leopold all together and licking them. He'd have just walked up to them and let them see that they'd jolly well better leave *him* alone in future. *He'd* have just laughed at that dog eating up all the pie. William promptly uttered a harsh sound and Cæsar cocked an ear and looked up apologetically. William was not a romancist for nothing. He had ceased to be William. Dick the Dauntless swaggered down the path to the gate with a dark scowl on his face.

Sam peered through the dusk.

'Well,' he said, eagerly. 'What 'v' you got?'

Through the bushes Cæsar swallowed the last mouthful of veal and ham pie and sat back with an expression of seraphic happiness, and Jumble humbly came forward to lick the dish.

'Nothin', you — you ole varlets,' cried Dick the Dauntless. 'An' I jolly well won't get anything, ever — till death — so there — an' you jus' clear off from outside my house, or I'll—'

He flung himself upon Sam. Sam, who was taken by surprise, rolled into the ditch. Albert and Leopold rushed upon William, Sam crawled out of the ditch to join them, and the battle began.

*

'It's gone,' said Mrs Brown. 'Simply gone.' The three men looked at her in bewilderment.

'The veal and ham pie,' exclaimed Mrs Brown. 'The one we were going to have for supper. Cook says she put it in the larder only two minutes ago, and now it's gone – simply gone. No one's been through the kitchen. Cook's been near the larder door all the time. Some tramp must have seen it through the window and taken it and—'

'He can't have gone far,' said Mr Brown.

Mr Beal sprang up.

'Let's catch him,' he said. 'He's probably eating it in the shrubbery now.'

The three men went out and gazed upon the darkening garden. A faint cracking of twigs in the shrubbery reached them. In single file and on tiptoe they set out. At last they discerned a dim figure in front of them carrying something in its arms and accompanied by a dog.

'There he is!'

'Quietly! We'll get him!'

'He's made friends with Cæsar!'

'Quite a small man.'

'Almost a boy.'

There was a horrible suspicion at the heart of William's father, but he followed with the rest. The figure disappeared behind a laurel bush. They followed, still on tiptoe. Behind the bush they found only Cæsar finishing the remains of the pie and Jumble watching him with wistful envy.

'Catch the old villain before he makes off,' said Mr Beal, and they hastened on to the hedge at the end of the garden and looked over it. There a glorious sight met their eyes. Dick the Dauntless was fighting for his life against hundreds of foes. He punched and butted and dodged and closed. Thousands fell at each stroke. He was dimly aware of three heads watching him over the hedge, but he had no time to look at them. He heard vague sounds, such as:

'Go it, William!'

'Get one in now, old chap!'

'Jolly good! Jolly good!'

'Give it 'em strong!'

Albert, with a bewildered cry of 'Oh, 'elp!' and a bleeding nose, began to run off towards home. There was very little left of Dick the Dauntless, but with a desperate effort he flung Leopold into the ditch, whence Leopold crawled forth and followed Albert. Only Sam was left. Sam was large and no coward, and, in spite of a bruised eye, would have kept up the fight longer had not Cæsar appeared.

One glance at Cæsar was enough for Sam. Echoing Albert's cry of 'Oh, 'elp!' he fled for dear life down the road. Then Dick the Dauntless vanished, and William, his collar burst, his tie streaming, his coat torn, his ear bleeding, turned to survey his audience of three from a quickly closing eye.

William, in his pyjamas, pondered for a moment over the mystery of human life as he bestowed those few perfunctory brushes upon his shock of hair that constituted its evening toilet. He had that day committed almost every crime known to boyhood.

He had brought 'common' boys home.

He had stolen a pie.

He had fought openly on the high road.

He had spoilt his collar and tie and coat, and acquired a thoroughly disreputable black eye.

Finally, turning from these crimes, fully expecting to meet with retribution at the hands of his family, he had been acclaimed as a hero. He was bewildered. He did not understand it. He did not know why he was a hero instead of a criminal. Anyway, it wasn't worth bothering over, and, anyway, he was going to have a jolly fine black eye, he thought proudly. He turned a somersault from his chair to his bed, which was his normal manner of entering it, and drew the clothes up to his chin. Before he finally surrendered to the power of sleep, he summed up his chief impressions of the evening.

'They're jolly queer, grown-ups are,' he said, sleepily. 'Jolly queer!'

CHAPTER 8
THE NATIVE PROTÉGÉ

The person who was ultimately to blame was the secretary of the Dramatic Society of the school of which William was a humble member. The Dramatic Society had given an historical play in which Christopher Columbus was depicted among the aborigines of America. William was too unimportant a member of the institution which served him out his daily ration of education to figure on the stage, but he was a delighted spectator in the back row. Christopher Columbus interested him not at all. Christopher Columbus was white, and except for his rather curious and violently anachronistic costume, looked exactly as the postman or William's own father might look. But the aborigines! William could not take his eyes from them. They were Jones Minor and Pinchin Major and Goggles, and all that crew. Of course he knew that. Yet how different – how rapturously different. Browned from head to foot – a lovely walnut brown. It made their eyes look queer and their teeth look queer. It set them in a world apart. It must feel ripping. William decided then and there that his life's happiness could never be complete till he had browned himself like that. He wondered whether brown boot polish would do it. Knife polish might. Something must.

He went out with the stream of spectators at the end in a golden dream of happiness. He saw himself, browned from head to foot, brandishing some weapon and dancing on bare brown feet in a savage land. He was so rapt in his daydream that he collided with a tall lank sixth-form boy who was coming along the passage carrying a box.

'Look out where you're going, can't you?' said that superior individual coldly. 'Do you want me to drop this stuff all over the place?'

He pointed with a languid hand to 'this stuff'. 'This stuff' was sticks of brown and red and black greasepaint, pots of cold cream, and tins of powder.

William's eyes brightened.

'Shall I carry it for you?' he said meekly. 'So's to save you trouble?'

The sixth-form boy started. William's attitude towards his intellectual superiors generally lacked that respect which is the due of intellectual superiors.

'Er – all right,' he said, handing the box to William and walking on down the passage.

William walked meekly behind with the box in his

arms. Very neatly as he turned the corner he transferred
two sticks of brown greasepaint from the tray to his own
pocket. He sternly informed his conscience (never a very
active force with William and quite easily subdued) as he
did so that he'd helped to pay for the beastly things, hadn't
he, anyway, by paying (or getting his mother to pay) two
shillings for a rotten seat in the rotten back row, where he
could only see by squinting round the feather in Dawson's
mother's hat, and anyway he'd like to know whose business it was but his. His conscience retired, completely
crushed.

At the door of the sixth-form room he handed the box
to the secretary of the Dramatic Society.

The secretary of the Dramatic Society entered the holy
sanctum.

'That young Brown's manners,' he remarked patronis-
ingly to his peers, 'seem to be improving.'

William surveyed the effect in the looking-glass. It was
perfect. He had completely used up the two sticks of
brown greasepaint upon the exposed parts of his person.
He found the question of clothing rather a difficulty. He
possessed no garment of the type that the aborigines had
worn, but his ordinary suit was, of course, unthinkable.
Football shorts seemed better – and a green football shirt

that had been Robert's. They partook in some way of the nature of fancy dress. Robed in them he surveyed himself again in the glass and a blissful smile stole over his cocoa-hued face. He was a perfect aborigine. It only remained to go out into the world to seek adventures.

Adventures came readily to William even when attired and coloured simply as a boy. He hardly dared to think what might happen to him as an aborigine – provided, of course, that he could get clear of the parental abode. Otherwise his mahogany career might come to an abrupt and untimely end. He looked cautiously out of the window. There was no one in sight. He lowered himself to earth by means of a tree that grew conveniently near his window.

'William!'

The voice came from the drawing-room.

William beat a hasty retreat into a clump of laurel and remained motionless.

'I'm sure I heard that boy . . . *William*!'

He decided to take the bull by the horns.

'Yes, Mother!' he called obediently.

'What are you doing?'

'I'm jus' sittin' in the garden an' thinkin', Mother,' said William, in a voice of honeyed wistfulness.

Mrs Brown, deeply touched, sought out her husband.

WILLIAM SURVEYED HIMSELF AGAIN IN THE GLASS, AND A
BLISSFUL SMILE STOLE OVER HIS COCOA-HUED FACE.

'You know, dear,' she said, 'there's something awfully sweet about William sometimes.'

William, having gained the open field, felt a sensation of extreme relief. For some time he crawled about in ditches tracking imaginary wild animals and scalping imaginary white men. Then the occupation began to pall, and he began to regret having carried off the coup in solitude. A few more aborigines might have been jollier. However, the brown was staying on all right, and that was a comfort. He left the fields and went into the woods. There he ran and leapt and climbed trees for a blissful half-hour. He also shot an entire menagerie of animals and slaughtered innumerable hosts of white men unaided. He went along the woods, then across three fields (by way of the ditches), and then down the valley, and then close by the side of a garden with which he was not previously acquainted. And it looked an interesting garden – just the sort of garden for an aborigine intent upon enjoying life to the full. He saw a shrubbery, an orchard, a stream, and some very climbable trees. He scrambled through a hole in the hedge to the detriment of the green football shirt and shorts. Then he ran riot in the jungle and along the sides of the raging torrent. In a fierce encounter caused by the joint attack of a lion and elephant and a rhinoceros (William did things upon a large scale) he ran (in pursuit, not in flight) to the further end of the shrubbery. There he was surprised to find an open lawn and a large concourse of people. The people sat in rows in chairs. There was something expectant in their expression. A tall man in black was standing in front of them with a watch in his hand. They were obviously waiting for something. When they saw William they rose as one man.

'*There* he is,' they said.

Before the bewildered William could realise what was happening they surrounded him on all sides and drew him on to the lawn. The clergyman held him by the hand.

'Don't be frightened, little boy,' he said kindly.

'I don't suppose he understands English,' said a tall, thin lady in a small sailor hat. 'They don't, you know – out there.'

A large motherly woman bore down upon him with a glass of milk and a bun. William was hungry. In moments of uncertainty his rule was to lie low and take the good things provided by the gods without question. Moreover, it was perhaps safer in the circumstances not to understand English – at any rate, not till he had consumed the bun and milk. They led him to a table facing the audience and put the bun and milk before him. People in the farther rows of chairs craned their necks to see him. He gave them his inscrutable frown in the intervals of drinking and consuming large mouthfuls of bun. The man stood up and addressed the gathering in a high-pitched, drawling voice.

'I need not inform my friends that we – er – see before us our – er – little protégé from Borneo and – er – let me say that he – er – does us credit.' He placed his hand upon William's head and looked down at William with a proud smile.

Meeting William's unflinching, unsmiling glare, his smile faded and he quickly drew back his hand.

'Er – credit,' he resumed, putting a hand to his collar as he moved a step farther from William, 'to – er – those who may be strangers here this afternoon let me say that we – er – of this – er – parish have – er – for the past two years – made ourselves responsible for the – er – rearing and – er – education of a little native of Borneo.'

He paused for applause, which was set going by the Vicar's wife, who was the tall, thin lady in the small sailor hat.

'The Reverend Habbakuk Jones, who is – er – at the native mission school, has come – er – over to see us – bringing – er – our little native protégé.' Again he smiled lovingly and drew near to William. William, whose mouth was fuller of currant bun than European etiquette would have sanctioned, raised his face, and, without interrupting the process of mastication, gave Mr Theophilus Mugg such a look as sent him precipitately to the farther end of the table.

'Er – protégé,' said Mr Theophilus Mugg uncomfortably. 'The Reverend Habbakuk Jones wrote this – er – morning to say that he would call with the – er – child' – he looked distrustfully at William – 'and leave him in our – er – loving care – while he – er – visited a relative in the – er – vicinity. He – er – promised to be – er – with us – by half past three to – er – deliver his address. He – er – evidently dropped his address. He – er – evidently dropped the – er – little boy – at the gate and – er – will soon be – er – present himself.'

He sat down as far away from William's eye as possible and wiped his brow. A crowd with a large preponderance of the feminine element gathered round William as he drained the last drop of milk. A fat, motherly woman handed him a piece of chocolate gingerly, as though he were a strange sort of wild animal.

'I wonder if he'll speak,' said someone wistfully.

'I expect he'll make some sort of thanks for the bun and milk and chocolates,' suggested someone else.

'Not in English, I expect,' said a third hopefully.

William rose to the occasion.

'Blinkely men ong,' he said clearly. There was a

murmur of rapt admiration.

'Hindustani, I believe,' said the Vicar's wife doubtfully. 'My father was in India several years.'

William soared to further heights.

'Clemmeny fal tog,' he said.

'The darling!' said the old lady. 'I'm sure he's saying something beautiful.' She held out a second slab of chocolate. 'I *love* those Eastern languages, so – *musical*.'

WILLIAM ROSE TO THE OCCASION. 'BLINKELY MEN ONG,' HE SAID CLEARLY.

'It's certainly Hindustani,' said the Vicar's wife. 'It all comes back to me.'

'Oh, what was he saying?'

'He was saying,' said the Vicar's wife, ' "Thank you for your kindness and food." '

'How beautiful!' said the fat lady, handing him a third slab of chocolate. 'I was taking this home for my son,' she explained, 'but I'd *much* rather give it to our dear little native protégé. Isn't it a beautiful thought that we reared and clothed him all this time?'

'I distinctly remember making that little green shirt,' said the Vicar's wife.

'Bluff iffn,' said William, who was growing bold.

'The angel!' said the fat lady. 'Doesn't it make you feel you'd do *anything* for him? What's his name?' she said to Mr Theophilus Mugg. 'I'd love to call him by his name.'

'I – er – am not sure of his name,' said Mr Theophilus Mugg with dignity.

'But wasn't it mentioned in the letter?'

'It was spelt,' said Mr Theophilus Mugg with increasing dignity. 'Needless to say, it was not pronounced. I have no wish to make myself ridiculous in the boy's eyes.'

'The mystery of these dark-skinned races,' said the Vicar's wife. 'The beautiful inscrutable faces of them. The *knowledge*, the *wisdom* they seem to hold.'

'Certainly it is not an English cast of countenance,' said Mr Theophilus Mugg.

'Bunkum allis lippis,' said William, feeling that something further was expected of him.

'Most *certainly* Hindustani,' said the Vicar's wife.

It was here that a small voice piped from the back row, 'It's William Brown!'

William, who was enjoying himself intensely, glared fiercely in the direction of the voice.

'Hush, hush, dear!' said the shocked voice of a parent. 'Of course it isn't William Brown. It's a poor little boy from a distant land over the sea – or India's coral strand,' she murmured vaguely.

'It *is* William Brown,' persisted the shrill voice.

'He may bear a resemblance to William Brown,' said the parent, 'but William Brown is white, I suppose, and this little boy is black.'

'Yes,' said a small, half-convinced voice, 'I s'pose so.'

They approached the table.

'My little girl,' said the parent pleasantly, 'sees a resemblance in the child to one of her schoolfellows.'

'Would you like to talk to the little boy?'

The little boy put out his tongue at her.

'A native form of greeting, doubtless,' said the Vicar's wife.

'Oo, it *is* William Brown,' persisted the little girl shrilly.

'If you say that again, dear,' said the parent, 'I shall have to take you home. It isn't kind. It may hurt the little boy's feelings. He's come a long, long way from a place where every prospect pleases and only man is vile, and you ought to be kind to him. How would you like to go to a strange faraway country and then have people say you were William Brown?'

This seemed unanswerable. The small child subsided.

Mr Theophilus Mugg looked anxiously towards the gate.

'He doesn't seem to be coming,' he said. 'Shall we – er – adjourn to the drawing-room for tea and – er – hear Mr Habbakuk Jones's – er – address afterwards?'

There was an animated murmur of acquiescence.

'The – er – child of the sun,' went on Mr Mugg, 'can stay out and we will – er – send his tea to him.'

William's expression brightened.

'Swishy,' he said.

'Thank you,' translated the Vicar's wife to the rest of the audience.

The small child had wandered round to the wake of William.

'He's not black all the way down,' she shrilled. 'He is—' She stopped abruptly, remembering the maternal threat. 'Well, anyway, he *is*,' she ended decidedly.

'Of *course* he must be black all the way down. Don't be silly,' said the parent.

'They *may* not be,' said an old lady with a kind face. 'Of course, one imagines they are, but, after all, one sees nothing but the exposed portions.'

At this point William, who was very hot, raised a hand to his brow to wipe away the perspiration. The sun was certainly having some effect upon his complexion. A pale patch followed the track of his hand. His hand in its downward journey rubbed upon his green shirt. A black patch followed its track. There was a sudden silence.

The Vicar's wife voiced the general sentiments.

'Curious!' she said.

'Surely,' said the old lady in a trembling voice, 'we haven't been imposed upon?'

'Impossible,' said Mr Mugg, pale but firm. 'I have known Mr Habbakuk Jones from childhood. He is incapable of deception.'

'Perhaps,' said the old lady, 'it's the effect of the sudden change of climate acting upon the pigment of the skin.'

There was a murmur of relief at the suggestion. William merely scowled at them. He was wondering how soon and on what pretest he could escape to the woods. He felt that he had exhausted the powers of entertainment of the present position, but he did not wish to miss the tea.

'We will not discuss the matter in the hearing of the child,' said Mr Muggs.

'But he doesn't speak English,' put in the old lady,

'He may *understand* it,' said Mr Mugg with dignity. 'Let us – er – discuss the matter over the – er – cup that cheers but not inebriates – ahem!'

Rather bewildered and looking back suspiciously at the inscrutable William, the company moved indoors. The old lady soon appeared with a heavily laden tray which she placed in front of William. She seemed about to make some kind remark, but meeting William's implacable frown, retired hastily.

'He's certainly beginning to look very annoyed,' she announced excitedly in the drawing-room.

'It is—' began the small shrill voice, then stopped abruptly.

It was just as William was consuming the last of a large plate of cakes that he noticed a couple of figures coming towards the house. One was a clergyman. The other was a boy about William's age, rather more swarthy than the average boy, and clad in an ordinary grey flannel suit. Nobody knew exactly what happened then. Certainly on that occasion William was *not* the aggressor. The new-comer may have disliked the look of William with his now streaky face and curious costume, he may have been hungry and found the sight of William, devouring the last cake, unbearable, he may simply have been feeling the heat. The fact remains that he hurled himself upon William with the agility of a wild cat, and William in sheer panic rushed through the open French window into the drawing-room, followed by his antagonist. The two of them charged through the crowded room. They left in their wake Mr Theophilus Mugg sitting upon a dish of cakes upon the floor, the Vicar's wife soaked in hot tea, the old lady mixed up with the fragments of a Venetian vase, and the parent of the child beneath the grand piano. Once outside the front door William doubled, threw off his pursuer and made for the woods.

He had made up his mind to go home and take the stuff off. It was coming off, anyway. It was possible that he might be home for tea. It was possible – he was rather doubtful about this, but determined to be optimistic – that his father might not come to hear of the affair. Anyway, it had been fun. It had been fun in the woods, and those old loonies had been fun, and the cakes had been scrummy.

In the garden peace was restored. The audience sat once more in orderly rows. At the table sat Mr Theophilus

Mugg, the Reverend Habbakuk Jones and the native protégé, now cool and peaceful and replete with cakes and milk. A name was being whispered from mouth to mouth among the audience. The Reverend Habbakuk Jones rose to his feet.

IN SHEER PANIC WILLIAM RUSHED THROUGH THE OPEN FRENCH WINDOW INTO THE DRAWING-ROOM, FOLLOWED BY HIS ANTAGONIST.

165

'Ladies and Gentlemen,' he began.

From the back now rose a shrill, excited voice. 'I *said* it was William Brown.'

CHAPTER 9

JUST WILLIAM'S LUCK

William had accompanied his mother on a visit to Aunt Ellen. Mrs Brown was recovering from an attack of influenza, and the doctor had ordered a change.

William did not accompany her because his presence was in any way likely to help her convalescence. On the contrary it was warranted to reduce any person of normal health to a state of acute nervous breakdown. He accompanied her solely because the rest of the family refused to be left in charge of him.

As his grown-up brother Robert somewhat ungraciously put it, 'Mother's ill already, and William can't make her much worse. It's no use getting the whole lot of us knocked up. Besides, Mother *likes* William.' He made the last statement in the tone of voice in which one makes a statement that is almost incredible, but true.

William was an entirely well-meaning boy. That fact must be realised in any attempt to estimate his character, but Fate had a way of putting him into strange situations, and the world in general had a way of misunderstanding him. At least, so it always seemed to William . . .

William was *bored* by Aunt Ellen, and Aunt Ellen's house, and Aunt Ellen's garden, and Aunt Ellen's cat, and Aunt Ellen's conversation, and Aunt Ellen's powers of entertainment.

Aunt Ellen had suggested many ways in which he might spend his first afternoon with her while his mother rested. He might sit in the garden and read. She'd rather he didn't go outside the garden alone, because he might meet rough boys, and she was sure his dear mother was most particular whom he met. So she gave him a book called *Little Peter, the Sunshine of the Home*, and put a chair for him in the garden.

'It's a beautiful book, William,' she said, 'and I think will do you good. It's a true book, written by the boy's mother, as the preface tells you. He is a beautiful character. I *love* the book, myself. We'll have a nice little talk about it when you've read it. It might prove the turning-point in your life. I'm sure you'll wish you knew Peter and his dear mother.'

William, after reading a few pages, began, as she had predicted, to wish he knew Peter and his mother. He wished he knew Peter in order to take the curl out of that butter-coloured hair and the fatuous smile from the complacent little mouth that stared at him from every illustration.

Driven at last to fury, he dropped Peter down the well, and began to look for more congenial occupations.

He tried to play with the cat, but the cat, not being used to William's method of playing, scratched him on the cheek and escaped under the bicycle shed, whither William could not follow him. William next climbed the apple tree, but; like the rest of Aunt Ellen's establishment, the apple tree was not 'used to boys', and the first branch upon which William took his stand precipitated him on to the lawn, and almost down the well, to join his victim, *Peter, the Sunshine of the Home*. Next he took up a few of Aunt Ellen's cherished chrysanthemums to compare the length of their roots at different stages, replanting them when he heard Aunt Ellen's footsteps approaching—

'William, darling,' she said reproachfully, 'have you finished the book?'

'Umph,' answered William non-committally.

'You must read very quickly, darling. I'll get you another. I have another book about Peter, you'll be glad to hear.'

William coughed politely.

'Thanks,' he said, 'I jus' don't feel like any more readin'. I'd like more to *do* somethin'. I'm tired of doin' nothin'.'

She looked at him helplessly.

'But what do you *want* to do, William darling?'

'Dunno. Any sort of a game would do,' he said graciously.

The only game in Aunt Ellen's house was an old archery set, a relic of her Victorian youth. She brought it down for William.

'You see, you shoot at the target, darling,' she explained.

'Thanks,' said William, brightening considerably. 'You needn't bother lending me the target.'

Aunt Ellen retreated upstairs to continue her interrupted nap.

It was only when William, in a perfectly laudable attempt to shoot an apple down from the apple tree, had broken the landing window, driven the cat into a hysterical state of fury, and landed an arrow full in the back of the next-door gardener, that Aunt Ellen raised herself once more from the bed that was usually the scene of such untroubled rest. She rescued William, in a state of indignation, from the cat and gardener, and suggested a little walk. She felt, somehow, less sure of the contaminating influence of the outside world on William's character.

'Everyone's got to *practise*,' said William indignantly. 'Well, I was only *practising*. I'd have got my eye in soon. I hadn't got my eye in when I hit 'em. Everyone's got to practise. No one's born with their eye in. If I went on about five minutes longer, I wouldn't be hittin' anythin' 'cept wot I wanted to. And then,' he added darkly, with a vague mental vision of the world in general, and Peter and the cat and the gardener in particular, at his mercy, 'then some folks had better look out.'

Aunt Ellen shuddered.

'Darling, don't you think a little walk would do you good?'

'I don't mind,' said William. 'May I take the bow and arrows?'

'I think not,' said Aunt Ellen.

'All right,' said William despondently.

William started off down the road. Aunt Ellen returned once more to her slumbers. Peace reigned once more over the house. But not over William. William walked slowly and dejectedly, his hands in his pockets. A week of sheer boredom lay before him – of a garden arranged purely for the grown-up world, of books containing obnoxious Peters, of irate gardeners, of spiteful cats. He didn't think that he was going to enjoy himself. He didn't think that there was going to be anything to do. He didn't think that his walk that afternoon would contain anything of the least interest.

He didn't know any boys here. He didn't want to know any boys in a place like this. They were probably all Peters. He felt a burning hatred of Peter. He wouldn't mind meeting Peter . . .

He was tired of walking along the high road. He crawled through a hole in the hedge and found himself in someone's garden. He didn't care. He was in the reckless mood of the outlaw. He walked along the lawn and up to the house. He didn't care. He'd like to see anyone try to turn him out. That ole gardener – that ole cat – that ole Peter. Then he stopped suddenly –

Through an open window he could see a room, and a man sitting at a writing desk. On the writing desk was a pile of books: *What to Do with Baby*, *Hints on the Upbringing of Children*, *Every Mother's Reference Book*, and others of the same nature. There were also several typewritten manuscripts and several copies of a magazine, *The Monthly Signal: A Magazine for Mothers*.

But it was not on these that William fastened his scowling gaze. It was on a book, or rather a pile of books, from whose covers the simpering, curly-haired face of the hateful Peter looked out upon the world.

The man who sat at the desk was reading a letter. There was a look of fear upon his face. Suddenly he looked up and met William's unflinching gaze. They stared at each other for a few moments, then the man put down the letter and ran from the room. Obviously it was the sight of William that had moved him. In a less defiant mood towards the world in general William might have taken to his heels. Now he stood his ground, frowning ferociously at the man as he came out of the front door. But his ferocity was not needed.

'I say,' began the man, 'do you live near here?'

William's frown did not relax.

'Stayin' here,' he admitted ungraciously.

'I say,' said the man again, 'could you help me? Just for this afternoon. I'll give you everything you want – a shilling, two shillings, ten shillings,' he went on wildly, '*anything*. You can come to this garden any day you like as long as you stay here. You can bird's-nest in the wood. I've got a boy's tricycle you can have and – you can do anything you like in the garden – there's a pond behind the house—'

'Can I have all those things you said, and do all those things you said?' said William guardedly.

'Yes – yes – if you'll do what I tell you just for this afternoon.'

'I'd do *anything* for those things,' said William simply.

'Come in,' said the man nervously. 'There's not much time. She'll be here any moment.'

'When she comes,' said the man quickly – 'she'll be here any minute now – I want you to pretend you're called Peter and I'm your mother – do you see?'

William was outraged.

'Me – Peter – *that boy?*' At his tone of contempt the man's eyes blinked.

'But he's a charming boy,' he said indignantly. '*Everyone* says so – I could show you letters—'

Only at the mental vision of the pond, the tricycle, the wood, the garden, the ten shillings, did William's conscience allow him to pocket his pride.

'He's more like a monkey out of the zoo than a boy,' he said bitterly. 'But I'll do it if you'll never tell anyone I pretended to be him.'

The man's pride was evidently wounded by William's attitude.

'I should have thought it an honour – I've had most flattering notices. I could show you letters. However, there's no time to argue – as I said, she may be here any minute. I shan't be here – you must see her alone – say you're Peter – I'm afraid you're the wrong type, sadly. Your hair doesn't curl and it's the wrong colour, and you're too big, and your expression's wrong – not sensitive enough, or gentle enough, or wistful enough—'

William was rather sensitive about his personal

appearance. He accepted it with resignation, as the subject of numberless jokes from his own family, but he resented comments on it from outsiders.

'All right,' he said coldly, 'if all that's wrong with me, you'd better get someone else wot's got his soft, silly face.'

'No, no,' said the man wildly. 'I didn't mean anything – and there's no time, I'm afraid, to procure a more sympathetic type. She may be here any minute – all I want is you to meet her and pretend to be Peter – I shan't be here – you must say that this is your home, and your mother's in bed with a bad headache, and is sorry she can't receive her – then she'll go away – come and tell me when she's gone away – see?'

'Umph,' agreed William.

A tall, angular figure was coming up the drive.

The man fled into the house with a groan.

Mr Monkton Graham was a literary man. That is to say, he wrote 'The Mothers' Page' for *The Monthly Signal: A Magazine for Mothers*. He signed it 'Peter's mother'. The page always centred round Peter.

'Peter's mother' told how she dealt with Peter's measles and whooping cough, and clothes, and temper (though Peter's disposition was really angelic), and how she arranged Peter's parties and treats and daily routine, and lessons and holidays, and how she influenced him for good with her sweet unselfishness and motherly wisdom, and what sweet things Peter did and said and thought. Peter was a decided cult. Mothers wrote to 'Peter's mother, care of the office, *Monthly Signal*', for advice about John, or Henry, or Jimmie, or even Ann.

Mr Monkton Graham was thinking of starting a Joan. Mothers sent flowers and photographs of John and Henry and Jimmie to him. Someone had even sent a tricycle to Peter. Mr Monkton Graham had written a letter of thanks in a round and childish hand. They asked for photographs of Peter. Mr Monkton Graham possessed an old photograph of a nephew of his. He had this 'touched up' and sent it out to Peter's admirers. It appeared in the magazine. The nephew was in South Africa, and would hardly have recognised it in any case. It created quite a furore.

At first Mr Monkton Graham's work had not been laborious. It had consisted of reading a paragraph in a standard reference book on the rearing of children, expanding it, Peterising it and adding the ineffably 'sweet' touch of 'Peter's mother' that earned him his six guineas a week. But success went to his head.

He wrote a book about Peter. It was wildly popular. He wrote another. It was still more wildly popular. He received letters and presents and photographs innumerable. They voted him a second 'Dearest' and Peter a second 'Fauntleroy'. He knew fame — even though a strictly incognito fame — at last. He always replied to his admirers — 'sweet' little letters, breathing the very spirit of 'Peter's mother'.

But last week, after a good dinner when he saw the world through a rosy mist, his usual discretion had deserted him. He had written to an admirer of Peter giving the name of the village and house where he lived. He had at the time not realised the significance of what he was doing. It only occurred to him the next morning when the letter was posted and the rosy mist had faded. The horrible thing had really happened. The woman had written to say that she was coming to see 'darling Peter's mother' that day. The letter had come by the midday post, and the visitor might be there any minute.

'We are not strangers, darling,' ran the letter; 'even as I write, though I have never seen you, I can see your fair curly hair — Peter's hair — and your dear blue eyes — Peter's eyes. When I think that I am going actually to see you two darlings, whom I feel I know so well, I can hardly believe my happiness. A kiss to you and darling Peter.'

As he had raised his anguished eyes from this letter, he had met the strange scowling face of a boy just outside his window. A gleam of hope came into his heart.

The situation might yet be saved. He might yet escape being held up to the scorn and ridicule of the readers of *The Monthly Signal: A Magazine for Women*. Looking again at the face of the boy, he had distinct misgivings, but he decided to try . . .

William remained at the front door till the tall, angular figure reached it. Then they stared at each other. William had a gift for staring. People who tried to stare him out soon realised their inferiority in the art.

'Good morning, little boy,' said the visitor.

'Umph,' replied William.

He was determined to earn that tricycle and pond and wood and birds'-nests and ten-shillings, and he felt that the less he committed himself to any definite statements outside his *role* the better.

'What's your name, dear?'

William inspected her. She looked harmless enough. She had a weak, good-natured face and greying hair and kind short-sighted eyes behind spectacles. She ought to be easy to make a mug of, thought William, out of the vast store of his knowledge of human nature.

'Peter,' he said.

The disappointment upon the good-natured face made William feel slightly annoyed.

'Peter? Surely not?' she quavered.

'That curly hair wot I had,' he explained, swallowing his annoyance, 'all came off – got clawered off by a monkey, at the zoo.' His imagination was coming to his aid as usual. 'I went too near the cage an' it stuck out its clawer an' clawered it all off – every bit. They took me home bald an' the nex' day it grew again but a bit different.'

'How terrible!' the visitor murmured, shutting her eyes. 'Wasn't your dear mother sad when it grew that colour?'

'No,' said William, coldly, 'she likes this colour.'

'That's so like her,' said the lady tenderly, 'to pretend to you that she likes it.'

William began to dislike the lady. He waited for her to continue the conversation.

'Somehow you're quite different in every way from what I expected,' she went on, with a distinct note of regret in her voice which William felt to be far from flattering. 'You're taller and stouter, and your expression . . . yes, that's QUITE different.'

'Yes,' said William, still anxious to carry out his part of the bargain. 'I've changed a lot since I had those pictures took. Got a bit older, you know, an' had some awful illnesses.'

'Really?' said the lady, in sympathy. 'Your dear mother never told me in her letters.'

'She never knew,' said William. 'I never told her, so as not to worry her. I jus' went about as usual, an' she never knew. But it made me look different afterwards.'

'It would,' said the lady, with a bewildered air. 'Well, shall we go in to your dear mother? She expects me, I believe. My name is Miss Rubina Strange.'

'Oh,' said William, 'she's ill. She said I was to tell you. She can't see you. She's very ill.'

'Ill? I am so sorry. But I would like to go to her. Perhaps I could do something for her.'

'No you can't,' said William, 'no one can. It's too late.'

'But – have you had the doctor?'

'Yes – he says it's too late to do anything.'

'Good Heavens! She's not—?'

'Yes, she's dyin' all right,' said William.

'But can't anything be done? This is dreadful! I feel absolutely heartbroken. I must just come into the house. There's surely something I can do!'

William followed her into the house. Mr Monkton Graham had not expected this. He was standing by the window of his study waiting till Miss Rubina Strange should depart. When he saw her about to enter the room, he did the only possible thing. He disappeared.

Miss Rubina Strange looked round the room with the air of a pilgrim visiting a holy place.

'And is this, dear Peter,' she said in a hushed whisper, 'where she writes those wonderful words?'

'Umph,' answered William.

'Oh, my dear! To think that I see it with my poor unworthy eyes. I have imagined it so often!'

Then she raised her long, thin nose, and sniffed.

'Peter, dear, there's just a faint smell of it . . . surely your dear mother doesn't smoke cigarettes?'

'No,' said William, absently, 'it was a pipe he was smoking.'

'Who?'

'Him,' said William, who was beginning to tire of the whole thing. It was the thought of the tricycle alone that upheld him.

'Your poor mind is unhinged,' said Miss Rubina, soothingly. 'I expect you are worrying over your mother's illness, which I'm sure you exaggerate, darling. I'm sure she'd have written to tell me if she'd been really ill. Is this the pen she writes with? And is this blotting-paper she's actually used? Peter, dear, do you think I could take just a corner of it – just a corner, just to remember my visit by for always?'

Mr Monkton Graham was growing uncomfortable. There was not really room under the table for a full-sized man to dispose his limbs. He stirred uneasily, and Miss

Rubina Strange turned startled eyes to William, placing her finger on her lips.

Then, snatching up the sacred pen she wrote on the sacred paper. 'Peter, there is a man underneath the table. Don't be alarmed. I am going to deal with him. Above all, do nothing to disturb your dear mother.'

William said nothing. He felt that the affair had got beyond him. Miss Rubina Strange crept cautiously about the room. She took a long narrow tablecloth from an occasional table, she took a length of picture-cord which she found in a drawer of the sacred writing desk, she took an ornamental dagger from a cabinet, she took a cushion from an armchair. Then she whispered to William, 'No noise or disturbance. Remember your mother is ill!'

Just as the innocent Mr Graham was trying to ease the ache in his neck by resting his head on his knee, he felt a sudden and violent attack in the rear. He was dragged out forcibly by a tall, thin female, who was nevertheless evidently possessed of unusual strength. Before he could remonstrate his feet were firmly tied together with a tablecloth, and he was half dragged, half helped to a sitting position on a chair. Then, leaning over him threateningly, with the dagger in one hand, the woman spoke.

'Make a sound,' she said in a low, hissing voice, 'utter one word, and I will strike. There is a sick woman in this

THE INNOCENT MR GRAHAM WAS DRAGGED OUT
FORCIBLY FROM HIS HIDING PLACE BY A TALL, THIN
FEMALE OF UNUSUAL STRENGTH.

house, and I will stop at nothing to protect her. You have
come to rob a woman who is a dear friend of mine, and
of every woman and, if necessary, I will take extreme
measures—'

Mr Graham looked apprehensively at the dagger. It
had, as he knew, a nasty sharp point. He therefore obeyed
her orders. He made no sound and uttered no word while

she tied the cushion over his face and pinioned his arms to his side with the picture-cord. Then she turned to William. William had for the moment lost all power of action. Things were moving too fast for him.

'She must know,' whispered Miss Rubina Strange. 'I'll break it to her gently. Don't let him move till I come back. I'll find out if she wishes to prosecute. Which is her bedroom?' He stared at her open-mouthed. 'Never mind,' she went on. 'I'll soon find her.'

When she had gone, William turned his gaze to the figure in the chair. All that could be seen above the pinioned arms was a large cushion. The cushion began to move spasmodically, to shake convulsively, and to utter muffled curses. The whole figure began to writhe in its bonds. From what he could make out of the words that came from the cushion, William instinctively felt that the monologue was one that his mother would not wish him to hear. He therefore listened attentively, mouth and ears wide open. The words appeared forcible if somewhat inaudible.

Just as Mr Graham had bent down his invisible head to try to bite the bonds round his knees through his cushion, Miss Strange, looking wild and dishevelled, returned.

'She's GONE . . .' she burst out. 'She's not in the

house, not in any of the bedrooms . . . What SHALL we do?'

At this point, with a bellow of rage, the man in the chair managed to shake off his cushion. The face that emerged was hardly human. Something violent had happened to its hair. Something violent had happened to its collar. Something violent had happened to its expression. Before he could utter anything that was in his mind, a housemaid came into the room.

'Oooo—' she said, 'it's the master. They're a-murdering of him! Ooo-oo!' With which remark she fled.

'The master!' gasped Miss Strange. She turned to William, 'I didn't know your father was alive.' Then she turned to the figure who was obviously seeking words capable of expressing his feelings. 'Where is your wife?' she ended sternly. 'Miserable man, where is your wife?'

'I haven't got any wife,' he shouted.

'But who wrote—'

'*I* wrote,' he yelled.

'Then Peter's mother—'

'There *isn't* any Peter's mother—'

'My poor man, have I touched on painful ground?' She placed a kind hand on William's head. 'Poor little orphan Peter,' she murmured softly. 'How long ago was it since she wrote to me?'

'There isn't any Peter,' shouted the man, like one distraught. 'There isn't any Peter's mother. There isn't any Peter. There isn't any Peter's mother. There's only ME, and you've nearly throttled me, and you've nearly suffocated me, and you've nearly knifed me, and would you mind going away? I don't know who the boy is,' he went on, following her gaze, 'except that he's some young ruffian trespassing in my garden, and who'll make my life a misery for the next few weeks till he kills himself or me, or I kill him or myself—'

Miss Rubina Strange, baffled for the first time that afternoon, sat down weakly.

'But I don't understand,' she said.

When she did understand, she did not sweep out of the room in disgust as he had hoped she would. Instead, she looked at him with bright eyes.

'But how *wonderful* of you,' she said. 'Of course, I will keep your dear secret. What sympathy and understanding of a woman's heart you have shown! It's all the more wonderful that you are a man. And we are friends, are we not? – old friends. We must have a chat.' She looked round the room. 'Let me tidy up a little first. Ah, the room needs a woman's touch . . . Then we will have a talk. There are so many things I want to ask and to tell you – ours will be a very beautiful friendship . . .'

Mr Monkton Graham threw a pathetic and pleading look at William.

'You may stay a little . . .' he said.

'Thanks,' he said coldly, 'I'd rather go jus' now. You won't forget those things you promised me, will you?'

'Er – no,' said Mr Graham, whose spirit was broken.

'My aunt's not got much of a garden,' said William, 'so I expect I shall be here most days. I'll come for the tricycle and money after tea.'

'We mustn't be shy of each other,' Miss Strange said in low, confidential tones; 'my friends call me Ruby . . .'

Mr Monkton looked wildly from her to William. His face was the face of a man in the depths of despair.

After tea, William's mother was anxious to know how William had spent his afternoon.

'I met a man,' he said casually, 'who's going to let me play in his garden an' he's given me a tricycle and some money.'

'Where does he live, dear?' said Aunt Ellen.

'At the end of the road,' replied William.

'Oh, I know,' said Aunt Ellen, 'it's a beautiful big garden. You're a very lucky boy, William. But I can't think why—'

'He must have taken a fancy to William,' said

William's mother. 'SOME people do . . .'

'Now I must find you something to read,' went on Aunt Ellen to William's mother. 'I've got some perfectly charming books that I know you'll love.'

'They're all about a little boy – such a dear – called Peter. They're written by his mother. They're perfectly true. She tells you so in the preface. They're so beautiful that they make me want to cry whenever I read them. I lent one to William before he went out this afternoon – *Peter, the Sunshine of the Home* – but he seems to have mislaid it. However, I've got heaps more. She – the mother – writes very beautiful little articles in one of the magazines. She must be a charming woman – to say nothing of Peter.' She threw William a smiling glance. 'There are some things our William might learn from Peter.'

With all his faults, William knew when to keep his own counsel.

He merely winked at the cat.

CHAPTER 10

THE GREAT DETECTIVE

The play was produced by the village Dramatic Society. William watched it spellbound from the front row, sitting between his mother and father. It was to him like the gateway to a new and enthralling life. He could not see why his elder brother and sister were laughing. The scene opened immediately after a murder. The corpse had been removed (somewhat to William's disappointment), otherwise the room was as the murderer had left it. William held his breath as innumerable uniformed policemen moved about the stage with notebooks, looking for clues, crawling under the table, and examining the floor with magnifying glasses. The only clue they could find left by the murderer had been a red triangle drawn upon a piece of paper and neatly pinned to the body by a dagger. This, they informed the audience many times, was the mark of a criminal gang of robbers and murderers who were baffling Scotland Yard.

Then the Great Detective came upon the scene, followed by a very bored-looking and elderly bloodhound, with its tail between its legs. The bloodhound, having made its appearance amid applause, contented itself with sitting in the corner of the stage and gazing scornfully at the audience. The Great Detective advanced to the centre of the stage, bent down, and picked up a cigarette end from the floor. It had been left by the murderer. The police, who had failed to notice it, fell into postures of ardent admiration. The cigarette end, naturally, bore the name of the maker, and yet more naturally was a blend made specially for the murderer. So justice set off hot upon the track, and the bloodhound yawned sleepily and shuffled off in the wake of the Great Detective.

The next scene showed the murderer moving in scenes of luxury and magnificence, wearing evening dress at all hours of the day, entertaining earls and ambassadors amid tropical palms and gilded pillars, and waited on by an army of obsequious footmen.

There was also the adventuress in a low (very low) red evening dress, smoking cigarettes upon a gilded settee. The plot was rather involved. There was a young man in a tweed suit, who kept appearing and calling to heaven to support his claim to the villain's place and wealth, which the villain himself dismissed with a most villainesque snarl. There was also a simple maiden in sky-blue muslin, with golden (very golden) hair, who was generally clinging to the young man or sobbing on his shoulder while he appealed to heaven to make him worthy of her.

But the Great Detective was the real hero of the play. He appeared (always in a dressing-gown) in his room smoking a pipe and working up clues, with his hand upon the collar of his amiable bloodhound, who tried to assure the audience by little deprecating wags of his tail that he wouldn't hurt a fly.

The last scene was the great excitement. The villain, still in evening dress, with his background of palms and pillars, was packing to go away. The Great Detective arrived, tore open his suitcase, and there were his handkerchiefs, adorned round the edges with red triangles – irrefutable proof – policemen with handcuffs spring from behind the palms – the young man, still wearing the young woman round his neck, appeared from nowhere and thanked heaven for bringing the guilty to justice – the bloodhound, in a sudden spasm of emotion, licked the villain's hand as he was led out, and all was over, leaving only the young man and young woman wringing the hand of the Great Detective, who was still wearing his dressing-gown and smoking his pipe.

William walked out of the hall in a dream. It all seemed so wonderful and yet so simple. Probably half the people one saw about were criminals and murderers, if only one knew.

You just found a clue and worked it up. It would be fine to be a detective. Of course, one needed a dressing-gown and a bloodhound, but he had a dressing-gown, and though Jumble wasn't exactly a bloodhound, he was a bloodhound as much as he was any kind of a dog. Jumble was all sorts of dog. That was what was so convenient about him.

Before William had retired to bed that night he had firmly made up his mind to lose no time in bringing some great criminal to justice with the aid of Jumble and his dressing-gown.

'There have been,' said Mrs Brown, William's mother, at breakfast the next morning, 'a lot of burglaries around here lately.'

William stiffened. A little later he went out, calling Jumble. He walked down the road, scowling at the houses as he went. In one of those larger houses the criminal must live, somewhere where there were palm trees and a butler. Of course, a murderer was more exciting, but a burglar would do to begin with.

He met a man coming up the road from the station, carrying a black bag. William glared at him suspiciously.

A bag! Of course a burglar would need a bag. Somewhat startled by William's stern, condemnatory expression, the man turned round again! William scowled still more. A guilty conscience! That was what made him turn round like that! He recognised, doubtless, the expression of a detective. Jumble barked excitedly, and wagged his tail. Even Jumble suspected something.

William turned and followed, creeping along in the shadow of the hedge, bent almost double. The man turned round again uneasily. William followed him till he

WILLIAM TURNED AND FOLLOWED, CREEPING ALONG IN THE SHADOW OF THE HEDGE, BENT ALMOST DOUBLE.

saw him enter a pair of large gates by the roadside and go up to a fair-sized house with large bow windows. William, with pride and determination writ large upon his freckled face, took a piece of chalk from his pocket and made a cross upon the stone gatepost. He had very neatly, and almost under the master's eye, removed the chalk from his master's desk at school that morning for the purpose. Becoming absorbed in his task, he turned the cross into a spider, and then into a shrimp. A few minutes later, inspired now purely by Art for Art's sake, he was adding a tree and a house, when he was roughly and ignominiously ordered off by a passing policeman. With a glance of crushing dignity, he obeyed.

If only that policeman knew—

That night, William, after retiring for the night, dressed himself completely, donned a dressing-gown in lieu of an overcoat, crept downstairs, and out of the back door. He released Jumble on his way.

Together they crept up the drive to the house. The bow window was open and the room was in darkness. The first thing William wanted to do was to find out what the inside of the house was like. If there were palms—

He climbed in by the open window, holding Jumble tightly beneath his dressing-gown. He went out of the room and across a hall past the open doorway of a room in which the man who had been carrying the bag was having dinner. Opposite him was (presumably) the adventuress – a little fatter than the adventuress in the play, and in a black evening dress instead of a red one. Still, you couldn't expect all adventuresses to look exactly the same. And she was wearing pearls. The pearls must be what the man had stolen last night and had been bringing home in his bag.

William stood in the doorway for a minute taking in the scene, then he went down to a room at the end of the passage – a glass room – *palms*! Ha! William had learnt all he wanted to know. He returned to the other room and out of the bow window.

That evening Mr Croombe, merchant in the city, turned to his wife, with a worried frown.

'There's something worrying me, old girl,' he said.

'What is it, Jim?' said Mrs Croombe.

'Well,' said Mr Croombe, throwing away his cigar end, 'have I seemed queer at all lately?'

'No,' said his wife anxiously.

'Not as if I might be subject to – er – hallucinations?'

'Oh no, Jim.'

'Well,' he said, 'it's a strange thing. I was coming along the road today – I suddenly saw a boy – I hadn't noticed him before, and he seemed suddenly to appear – a most peculiar expression – most peculiar – very intense and searching, as if he had some message – you know, I'm never quite sure that there's nothing in spiritualism. Well, I kept thinking about it as I changed – that peculiar piercing expression – wondering, you know, whether it was hallucination or a message, or anything, you know. There was something not *ordinary* about his expression, and,' he was obviously reaching the climax of the story – 'well, you may hardly believe me, but – this evening, as we sat at dinner, I looked up and distinctly *saw* the same boy standing in the doorway and looking at me again with that peculiar expression. He wore a strange flowing garment this time. I pinched myself and looked round the room, and then, again at the door, and he'd disappeared. Yet I swear I saw him, with just that extraordinary expression, looking at me – just for a minute.'

Mrs Croombe, open-mouthed, laid aside her sewing.

'My *dear* Jim!' she said. 'How extraordinary! I wonder – you might try psychoanalysis if the vision comes again – it's quite fashionable!'

'I hope,' said Mr Croombe, 'that it won't appear again. It wasn't,' he confessed, 'on the whole, a pleasant expression.'

Meanwhile, William, asleep in bed, was dreaming of

Mr and Mrs Croombe, handcuffed, and dressed from head to foot in red triangles.

'It's chiefly jewellery that's been taken,' announced Mr Brown from the local paper the next morning at breakfast.

'Ha!' said William sardonically.

'Mrs Croombe wants us to go to dinner on Saturday,' said Mrs Brown, looking up from a letter.

'Who's Mrs Croombe?' said Ethel, William's elder sister.

'They're new people, up Green Lane, the end house!'

'Ha!' snorted William.

'What,' said William's elder brother, 'is the matter with *you*?'

'You'd like to know, wouldn't you?' said William with a disrespectful contortion of his face. '*Just!*'

Then he went up to his bedroom and, putting on his dressing-gown, stood scowling into space with his head resting on his hand and his elbow on the mantelpiece in the attitude of the Great Detective thinking out a clue.

The bloodhound insisted on spoiling the picture by sitting up to beg.

That evening Mr Croombe looked very weary when he came home.

'I went to a psychoanalyst,' he said wearily, 'about that – boy, you know, and he asked me questions for over an hour – all about my past life. He asked me if I'd ever had a shock connected with boys, and I remembered that squib that a boy let off just in front of me last November. He says that this hallucination may be caused by a sub-conscious fear. He gave me a lot of other cases of the same kind that he's treating. He says that if, when I see the boy, I try to remember that really he doesn't exist, I may get over it. I met cousin Agatha afterwards. She thinks it's a message – she wanted me to ask the Psychical Research Society to come down, but I think I'll wait till after the dinner-party anyway.'

Mrs Croombe clasped her hands.

'Oh, Jim!' she said. 'It's all very wonderful, isn't it?'

William, after deep consideration, had decided not to take anyone into partnership. In the play there had been a faithful and unobtrusive friend of the Great Detective, who had merely asked questions and expressed admiration, but William, reviewing his circle of friends, could not think of anyone who would be content with this role. Therefore, he kept the whole thing to himself. He decided to bring off his great coup on the evening of the Croombe's dinner-party. He decided to go into the house and hide till the dinner had begun, and then go out and collect the stolen jewellery and convict the criminals. He expected vaguely to be summoned to Buckingham Palace to receive the VC after it. Anyway, his family would treat him a bit different – *just*!

He was in his bedroom, wearing his dressing-gown, and his faithful bloodhound was worrying the cord of it. He was sucking a lead pencil to represent the Great Detective's pipe. He had, at an earlier stage, experimented upon an actual pipe removed from the greenhouse where the gardener had left it for a moment. A very short experience of it had convinced him that a lead pencil would do just as well.

Dusk was already falling when the Great Detective issued forth – a sinister figure, with frown, lead pencil and dressing-gown – on the track of the criminals. The villain's house was brightly lit up, and he experienced some difficulty in making his way in. He made it ultimately through the larder window, and was detained for a few minutes by a raspberry cream which was a special weakness of his. Then, leaving the empty plate behind him, he gathered his dressing-gown about him and reconnoitred. The coast seemed to be clear. He crept upstairs and then on all fours along the landing. A door opened suddenly, and the master of the house, in shirt-sleeves, appeared full in William's way. William returned his gaze unflinchingly. The master of the house paled and retired precipitately to his wife's bedroom.

'I've seen it again, Marie,' he said.

'What, dear?'

'The – er – subconscious fear – the – er – message, you know. It was crawling along the passage outside in its curious long garment, and it gave me just the same kind of

WILLIAM RETURNED HIS GAZE UNFLINCHINGLY. THE
MASTER OF THE HOUSE PALED AND RETIRED
PRECIPITATELY.

look. *Piercing*, you know – almost hostile. I'm beginning to feel rather nervous, my dear. You've – never seen anything of it, have you?'

'Never!'

Mr Croombe wiped the perspiration from his brow.

'I'd better look up some sort of comfortable – asylum, you know, somewhere where the food's good – in case I go clean off it suddenly. I believe it generally begins by hallucinations.'

'You must go away for a change,' said Mrs Croombe firmly, 'as soon as you can after the upset of this party's over.'

'Yes,' said Mr Croombe, 'but supposing I see it *there* – when I have gone away?'

'I don't know,' said Mrs Croombe vaguely. 'Perhaps they don't travel – hallucinations, I mean.'

Meanwhile, the hallucination itself was concealed under the bed of his victim. He waited till host and hostess had gone down. He heard the sound of effusively polite greetings downstairs.

'How *good* of you to come!'

'Ha!' snorted William to a cardboard hat-box that shared his refuge with him. 'Just you *wait*!'

Then he crept out and began to look around the room. He managed to find some of Mr Croombe's handkerchiefs and was disappointed not to find red triangles on them, but he found a horseshoe on one, and that was just as likely to be the sign of a criminal gang. Then he went through the connecting door to Mrs Croombe's bedroom. He opened a drawer and saw a leather box. There was a key in it, but it was not locked. He opened it – pearls, rubies, emeralds – *all* the stolen jewellery.

'Ha!' said William.

He emptied it into the pocket of his dressing-gown. He looked round the room again. There were some silver boxes and candlesticks. William's stern frown deepened.

'Ha!' he said again.

All stolen things. He put them also in his pockets.

The next thing was to try and find some handcuffs somewhere. He ought to have thought of that before.

The party downstairs was going very well. The conversation turned on the thefts in the neighbourhood.

'I hear that they have taken a considerable amount of jewellery,' said Mrs Brown.

Mrs Croombe paled.

'Jewellery!' she said. 'Jim! I believe I forgot to lock my jewel-case. I believe I just left it in my drawer.'

He rose.

'I'll go and see, dear,' he said.

He went out of the room. At the foot of the stairs was William, in a conspiratorial attitude, his pockets bulging.

White to the lips, Mr Croombe returned to his festive board.

'I can't go just now, dear,' he said to his wife, then he whispered with an air of mystery:

'*It's* there!'

AT THE FOOT OF THE STAIRS WAS WILLIAM, IN A
CONSPIRATORIAL ATTITUDE, HIS POCKETS BULGING.

Someone gave a little scream.

'Oh, is the house haunted?'

'Well,' admitted Mr Croombe, not without a certain wistful pride, 'it's not exactly the house. To be quite precise, it's I who am haunted.'

The whole table was agog.

'It's – a boy,' said Mr Croombe. 'I see him everywhere – in the road, in the house, with a *piercing* expression and curious raiment. He looks straight *at* me as if he meant something – a sort of freckled face – not friendly, I'm afraid. I've been psychoanalysed. It's a sort of – er – complex—'

There was a hubbub of excitement.

'Is it there – now – outside the room?'

'It *was*, but *anyone* mightn't see it.'

'May we go and see?'

'Er – yes. I should think so – but be careful. You know, those – er – emanations can be very dangerous – a hostile aura, you know.'

Three or four bold young men opened the door and crept cautiously into the hall. There was the sound of a scuffle and a high, indignant voice, familiar to two at least of the guests. The jaws of Mr and Mrs Brown dropped suddenly.

'Let *go* of me! Take your ole hands *out* of my pocket.

Mind your *own* business! Well, I'm a detective, but I've not got any handcuffs. Leave *go* of me – I've left my blood-hound behind – that's not *your* stuff – well it isn't his'n'— it's stole stuff. I've tooken it 'cause I'm a detective – let *go* of me, I say. Leave go of my dressing-gown, will you? I'll call the police – I say he's a robber, an' I bet he's a mur-derer – will you let *go* of me? He's a gang – look at his handkerchiefs – what d'you think of that – well, will you let *go* – ?'

Still expostulating, William was dragged into the dining-room. Mr Croombe covered his face with his hands.

'That's it,' he said. 'Don't bring it too near.'

'It's the thief,' said the young men excitedly. 'Look at his pockets full of things!'

'Leave *go* of me!' said William, with rising irritability.

'My jewels!' screamed Mrs Croombe.

Mrs Brown, meeting her son face to face in such cir-cumstances, did the only possible thing. She fainted dead away and did not recover till the crisis was partially over.

William frenziedly accused Mr Croombe of theft and murder. He referred to handcuffs and bloodhounds. He said wildly that he had had the house surrounded by police. It took about half an hour to convince him of his mistake.

'How do you *know* they're their own things? They only *say* so – I've seen him walking suspicious with a bag full of something. Well, how do you *know* he isn't a gang?'

William, at the head of the gaily decorated table, pale and determined, in his dressing-gown, gesticulated wildly with his hands full of jewellery.

Mr Croombe was apologetic and pleading, wistfully grateful to William for being real.

William – only gradually, and under the influence of a large and indigestible meal which Mr Croombe insisted on giving him in proof of his gratitude – forgot his grievances.

Later, he found his father less sympathetic. Later still, he surveyed the world scornfully through his bedroom window, and thought of his family. It was no good trying to do anything with a family. The only thing was to cut loose from it altogether.

Mentally he surveyed the past evening. Everything was different in real life. What was the good of being a detective when everybody said the people hadn't done the things?

Real life was stupid.

He decided to go on the stage. There one could be a detective in comfort, and everyone didn't say the person hadn't done the things, and you'd made a mistake.

He'd go on the stage.

Feeling much comforted by this resolve, he got into bed and went to sleep.

CHAPTER 11

THE CIRCUS

The circus was to be held in a big tent on the green. William had watched them putting up the tent the day before. He had hung around with wistful eyes fixed upon it. Here was the Wonder of Wonders, the Mystery of Mysteries – a circus. He had seen the posters of it. It would be there that very day, with its lions and tigers, its horses and dogs, its golden-haired, short-skirted beauties, its fascinating red-nosed kings of laughter, its moustached masters of the ring, its quips, its thrill, its mystery, its romance, its gilt and tinsel and light – a circus! It is a strange fact that William had lived for the eleven years of his life and never seen a circus. But he was determined that the omission should be rectified. It was dusk when he saw them pass. Through the bars of the cages looked out weary, spiritless lions and tigers, but to him they were veritable kings of the jungle. There was an elephant and two camels, and, chained to the top of the van, a monkey, shivering in a green jacket.

'Gosh!' ejaculated William in rapture and admiration.

There were several closed vans, but to William it was as if they were open. Clearly in imagination he saw the scene within. There sat laughing clowns and beautiful women with filmy skirts that stuck out round their knees. He could imagine the clowns pouring forth an endless succession of jokes, each with suitable contortions. The beautiful women would be laughing till their sides ached. He wished he had a clown for a father. Imagination almost faltered at the blissful thought. A ragged man leading one of the horses looked curiously at him – a small boy leaning against a lamp post with all his soul in his eyes.

Slowly and reluctantly he went home to supper and bed. He dreamed of horses and lions, and tigers and clowns, and a life of untrammelled joy and jollity.

'There's a circus on the green,' he announced at breakfast.

'Don't talk with your mouth full,' ordered his father.

William looked at him coldly. A clown would not have said this. He wondered on what principle parents were chosen. He sometimes wished he had been given some voice in the choosing of his. There were one or two improvements he could think of. He swallowed with slow dignity. Then: 'There's a circus on the green,' he announced again.

'Yes, dear,' said his mother soothingly. 'Ethel, pass the marmalade to your father. What were you saying, dear?'

Whereupon William's father proceeded with a monologue upon the Labour question that he had begun a few minutes previously. William sighed. He waited till the next pause.

'I'm *goin'* to the circus,' he announced firmly.

That brought their attention to him.

'I don't see how you can, dear,' said his mother slowly. 'It's only staying for this afternoon and evening, and it's the dancing class this afternoon—'

'*Dancin'!*' repeated William in horror. 'Shurly you don't expect me to go to *dancin'*, with a circus on the green?'

'I've paid for the twelve lessons,' said Mrs Brown firmly, 'and Miss Carew is very particular about your not missing without a real excuse.'

'Well, there's this evening,' said William.

'You know Grandfather and Aunt Lilian are coming,' said Mrs Brown, 'and they'd be most hurt if we went out the first evening.'

'Well, they're comin' to stay a *week*,' said William with the air of one who exercises super-human patience; 'shurly they won't mind if I'm out for *one* night? Shurly they aren't as fond of me as all that? I should think Aunt Lilian would be *glad* I'm out from the things she said about me last time she came. You know she said—'

'You can't go alone,' said Mrs Brown wearily. 'It doesn't begin till eight. It's an absurd hour to begin. You can't stay up so late, for one thing, and you can't go alone, for another—'

'Why NOT?' said William with growing exasperation. 'Aren't I *eleven*? I'm not a *child*. I—'

William's father lowered his newspaper.

'William,' he said, 'the effect upon the nerves of the continued sound of your voice is something that beggars description. I would take it as a personal favour if it could kindly cease for a short time.'

William was crushed. The fact that he rarely understood his father's remarks to him had a good deal to do with the awe in which that parent was held. Clowns, he thought to himself smoulderingly, didn't say things that no one knew what they meant. Anyway, he was going to that circus. He finished his breakfast in dignified silence with this determination fixed firmly in his mind. He was going to that circus. *He was going to that circus.*

'Fold up your table napkin, William.'

Slowly and deliberately he performed the operation.

'I bet clowns don't have the beastly things,' he remarked dispassionately.

With which enigmatical remark he departed from the

211

bosom of his family. He was escorted to the dancing class in the afternoon by his elder sister Ethel. He signified his disgust at this want of trust in him by maintaining a haughty silence except occasionally unbending so far as to ejaculate in a voice of scornful indignation, '*Dancin'!* Huh! – *Dancin'!*'

During the dancing class his attention wandered. Miss Carew's patience changed gradually to wearied impatience.

'Slide the right foot, children, *right* foot, William Brown! Now chassé to the left. I said *left*, William Brown. Now three steps forward. *Forward*, William Brown. I didn't say stand still, did I? Now, take your partner's hand – your *partner's*, William Brown – Henry is not your partner.' William's real partner glared at him.

William performed evolutions tardily, faultily, and mechanically. He saw not a roomful of small boys and girls, shining with heat and cleanliness, dominated by Miss Carew's commanding voice and eager gaze. He saw not his own partner's small indignant face; he saw a ring, a ringmaster, a clown, lions, tigers, elephants – a circus!

He was aroused by a sudden wail from his small partner. 'I don't want to dance wif William! I don't like dancing wif William. I want to dance wif someone else. William does everyfin' wrong!'

William gazed at her with a reddening countenance. The dancing class stopped dancing to watch. The maiden found a small handkerchief hidden in a miniature pocket and began to sob into it. 'I could dance *nice* wif someone nice. I can't dance wif William. He does it all wrong.'

'*Me?*' said William in horror. 'I've not done anything. I dunno what she's cryin' for,' he explained to the room helplessly. 'I've not done nothin' to her.'

'You're enough to make any little girl cry,' said Miss Carew sharply, 'the way you dance!'

'Oh, *dancin'*,' said William scornfully. Then, 'Well, I do it all right in the end. I'm only a bit slow. I'm thinkin' of sumthin' else, that's all. That's nothing for her to cry for, is it? Cryin' because other people dance slow. There's no sense in that, is there?'

The sobs increased. It was a warm afternoon, and Miss Carew's exasperation changed to a dull despair.

'Will any kind little girl take William Brown for a partner, and give Mary a rest?'

There was no answer; William was aware of a distinct sense of mortification.

'Well, I don't *want* any of 'em,' he said huffily. 'I'll dance slow by myself. I'd sooner dance by myself than with an ole cryin' girl. I'll' – a brilliant idea struck him –

'I'll go home, shall I? I shan't mind going home.' His cheerfulness grew. 'Then she,' he indicated his late partner, 'can do it quick by herself and give up cryin'. I'll go home. I don't mind goin' home.'

'No, you *won't*,' said Miss Carew. 'I'll give – I'll give a chocolate to any little girl who will dance with William Brown.'

A stout little girl, famed for her over-indulgence in sweets, volunteered. William received her with an air of resigned patience.

'Well, don't *cry* over me,' he said sternly. She was less disposed to suffer in silence than his previous partner.

'He's treading on my toes,' she announced in shrill complaint when the dancing was once more in full swing.

The goaded William burst forth. 'Her feet are all over the place. I can't keep *off* them. She moves them about so quick. She puts them just where I'm going to tread on purpose. I don't *want* to tread on her ole feet. Well, I can't do what you say and not tread on her feet, 'cause when I do my feet, how you say do them, they go on her feet 'cause she's got her feet there first 'cause she's quicker than me an'—'

Miss Carew raised her hand to her brow.

'William,' she said wearily, 'I really don't know why you learn dancing.'

'I learn dancin',' said William bitterly, ''cause they *make* me.'

The various tribulations of the dancing class almost drove the thought of the circus from his head. But he saw the tent as he went home. It was in darkness, as the afternoon performance was over, and the only sign of life he could see was a thin dog chewing a turnip at the tent door. He supposed that the clowns and princess-riders were having tea in the brilliantly lit interiors of the closed caravans. He could imagine their sallies of wit and mirth; he listened for their roars of laughter, but the caravan walls were thick and he could hear nothing but a noise that might have been a baby crying, only William supposed it could not be that, for no baby who was lucky enough to live in a circus could surely be so misguided and ungrateful as to cry.

'I guess no one ever made *them* learn dancin',' he said feelingly.

He found that Grandfather Moore and Aunt Lilian had already arrived.

William had never met his grandfather before, and he gazed in astonishment at him. He had met old people before, but he had not thought that anything quite so old as Grandfather Moore had ever existed or ever could exist. He was little, and wrinkled, and shrivelled, and bald. His face was yellow, with tiny little lines running criss-cross all over it; his bright little eyes seemed to have sunk right back. When he smiled he revealed a large expanse of bare gum, with three lonely-looking teeth at intervals. He had a few hairs, just above his neck at the back, otherwise his head was like a shining new egg. William was fascinated. He could hardly keep his eyes off him all tea-time.

Aunt Lilian's life work was looking after Grandfather Moore. It filled every minute of her time. She was a perfect daughter.

'May he sit with his back to the light?' she said. 'You know you're better with your back to the light, dear. Bread and milk, please. Yes, he always has that, don't you, dear? Are you quite comfortable? Wouldn't you like a cushion? Get that footstool, William. This is William, dear – little William.'

'William,' he repeated, and smiled.

William felt strangely flattered.

'He's getting a bit simple,' sighed Aunt Lilian, 'poor darling!'

She was firm after tea.

'You'll go to bed now, dear, won't you? You always like to go to bed early after a journey, don't you? He always likes to go to bed early after a long journey,' she explained to the company.

She helped him upstairs tenderly and left him in his room.

William was despatched to bed at half past seven as usual. They were surprised at his meekness. They thought he must have forgotten about the circus. They carefully avoided all mention of it. But William's silence was the silence of the tactician. Open attack had failed. He was now prepared to try secrecy.

Up in his room he sat down to consider the most unostentatious modes of exit from the house. There was the possibility of going downstairs and through the hall on stockinged feet so quickly as to escape notice. But there was always the chance of somebody's coming out into the hall at the critical minute, and then all would be lost. Or there was the possibility of climbing down from his window, but his room was on the third storey, and he had never yet attempted a descent from that height. Just beneath his room was Grandfather Moore's room. From the window of Grandfather Moore's room an old fig tree afforded a convenient ladder to the ground. Grandfather Moore had gone to bed directly after tea. He would surely be asleep now. Anyway, William decided to risk it. He crept down the steps to Grandfather Moore's room and cautiously opened the door. The room was lit up, and before the fire sat Grandfather Moore, fully dressed. It was now impossible to withdraw. The bright little eyes were fixed on him, and Grandfather Moore smiled.

'William!' he said with pleasure. Then, 'I've not gone to bed yet.' He was obviously revelling in his wickedness.

William came in and shut the door.

'Can I get through your window?' he said shortly.

'Yes,' said Grandfather Moore. 'Where do you want to get to?'

'I'm going to a circus,' said William firmly.

The bright eyes grew wistful.

'A circus!' said the little old man. 'I went to a circus once – years and years ago. Horses and elephants and—'

'Lions an' tigers an' camels an' – an' – an' clowns,' supplied William.

'Yes, clowns,' said the old man eagerly. 'I remember the clown. Oh, he was a funny fellow! Are you going alone?'

'Yes,' said William, crossing to the window.

'Do they know you're going?'

'No.'

The little old man began to tremble with excitement.

'William – I want to see a circus again. Let me come too.'

William was nonplussed.

'You can't climb down this tree,' he said judicially. 'I was goin' climbin' down this tree.'

'I'll go downstairs,' suggested Grandfather Moore. 'You wait for me outside. I'll come out to you.'

But William's protective interests were aroused.

'No; if you're goin', I'll stay with you.'

He found the old man's hat and coat and helped him on with them. The old man was quivering with eagerness.

'There will be a clown, won't there, William? There *will* be a clown?'

'I *know* there's a clown,' William assured him.

They crept downstairs and through the hall in silence. Fortune favoured them. No one came out. Mr Brown, Mrs Brown, Ethel and Aunt Lilian were playing bridge in the drawing-room. The hall door stood open.

Outside Grandfather Moore gave a wicked chuckle.

'Lilian – she thinks I'm in bed,' he said.

'*ShH!* Come on!' whispered William.

Outside the tent door he remembered suddenly that he possessed no money. His last penny had been spent on a bag of popcorn the day before. Grandfather Moore was crestfallen. He said he had no money, but a systematic search revealed a shilling in the corner of his coat pocket, and his face lit up.

'It's all right, William,' he said gleefully.

A stream of people were entering the tent. There was the ring, the sawdust, the stands for the horses, the sea of

THEY CREPT DOWNSTAIRS AND THROUGH THE HALL IN
SILENCE.

people, the smell that is like no other smell on earth – the smell of the circus! William's heart was too full for words. He could hardly believe his eyes. It was all too wonderful to be true. And there in the ring was a clown – a jolly, red-nosed, laughing clown. Grandfather Moore clutched his arm.

'The clown, William!' he gasped in ecstasy.

William sighed – a deep sigh of intense happiness.

They secured good seats in the second row from the bottom and sat in silence – a curious couple – their eager eyes fixed on that figure o' dreams with a loose white suit and a chalked face. He held a small camera and he was offering to take the photographs of the people who came in. At last a farmer and his wife agreed to be photographed. He posed them carefully in the middle of the ring, the lady in a chair, her hands folded in her lap, the man standing by her side, his hand on her shoulder. Then he told them not to move. He said he was going to photograph them from behind first. He went behind and disappeared through the door of the tent. The couple stayed motionless with sheepish grins on their faces. The suppressed titters of the audience increased to roars of laughter. It was some time before the rustic couple realised that the clown was not photographing them carefully from behind. William enjoyed the joke. He emitted guffaw after guffaw while Grandfather Moore's shrill cackle joined in.

'He's gone away, William!' he piped between his laughter. 'He's gone right away! They think he's taking them from behind!'

At last the joke dawned upon the bucolic couple, and they went to their places amid applause.

Then began the circus proper. The ring-master came on – a magnificent creature with long moustachios and a white shirt front. He waved his whip. Then all held their breath, for in there pranced a coal-black horse, and on its back one of the visions of beauty, whose pictures had been on the poster – golden hair, red cheeks, white tights, and short, white, frilly skirts.

To William she was Beauty personified. In the fickleness of his youth he decided not to marry the little girl next door after all. He would marry her instead. He would be a clown and marry her. He watched her with fascinated eyes. She rode round the ring bareback – she then rode round standing on the horse's back and blowing them kisses. William blushed violently when he imagined one came to him.

'Golly!' he breathed.

'Isn't she fine?' said Grandfather Moore.

'Isn't she *just*?' said William.

All the while the majestic ring-master stood in the centre of the ring twirling his moustachios and flicking his long, curling whip.

Then a man brought her a white horse, and she raced round the ring, leaping gracefully from horse to horse at full gallop. Oh, the dreadful moment when William thought she might fall. He would have leapt from his seat

SHE RODE ROUND THE RING BAREBACK – BLOWING THEM
KISSES. WILLIAM BLUSHED VIOLENTLY WHEN HE IMAGINED
ONE CAME TO HIM.

and saved her, dying, perhaps, in the attempt. His thoughts lingered fondly on the scene. Then she leapt through the paper hoop again and again, landing gracefully upon the black or white back. William grew impatient for the time when he should be old enough to be a clown and marry her. The thought of the dancing class had faded altogether from his mind. The thoughts of youth may be long, long thoughts, but its memories are distinctly short.

Then the clown came on again. How they roared at him. He tried to get on to a horse and he couldn't; he tried to stand on a chair and he couldn't; he tried to do conjuring tricks and he dropped everything; he tried to walk across the ring and he slipped at every step. He fell over his trousers; he fell over the ring-master; he quarrelled with the ring-master; the ring-master knocked him down; he said the funniest things William had ever heard in all his life. William was literally exhausted with laughing; Grandfather Moore was hoarse. Occasionally his cackling laugh cracked feebly on the top note.

Open-mouthed and tense they watched a collie dog carry in its puppy, nurse it, give it a bottle of milk and put it in its cradle; watched the elephant pick out numbers at the direction of the ring-master; watched the monkey ride a bicycle and pelt the clown with sawdust. But the last item was the most stupendous. It was called 'The Prairie on Fire'. There were real flames – red, rolling flames; and through them, and in headlong flight before them, came cattle and horses and buggies, whose occupants stood up lashing on the horses and casting glances of terror at the flames. The golden-haired beauty was wringing her hands in the last buggy but one. The monkey was on the seat with the driver.

'Crumbs!' gasped William.

Grandfather Moore was beyond words.

Almost dazed and drunk with happiness they went out into the darkness at the end. They walked in silence till they were almost at the gate of William's house.

Then William spoke.

'I don't care what they do to me. It was worth it – jolly well worth it.'

Grandfather Moore gave a chuckle.

'That *was* a circus, William! I saw a fine one when I was a boy too. I didn't care what I did to get to a circus.'

William felt that he had found a kindred spirit.

'Did you learn dancin'?' he asked with interest.

'Yes.'

'Did you like it?'

'*No*,' said Grandfather Moore emphatically.

The bond between them grew stronger.

The hall and staircase were empty as they crept cautiously in through the front door. Mr Brown, Mrs Brown, Ethel and Aunt Lilian were still playing bridge in the drawing-room. Silently, on tiptoe, they crept upstairs to bed.

Mrs Brown was apologetic at breakfast.

'I was so sorry about the circus, dear,' she said to William. 'It just came on an awkward day when no one could take you. There's sure to be one again soon. You shall go to that.'

'Thank you, Mother,' said William, his eyes fixed upon his plate.

'You didn't mind very much, did you, dear?' she continued.

'No, Mother,' said William meekly.

Aunt Lilian beamed across at her charge.

'*Doesn't* he look well this morning? I don't know *when* I remember him looking so well. A good long night does him no end of good. I'm so glad I persuaded him to go to bed directly after tea.'

William's eyes and Grandfather Moore's eyes met for a second across the table.

CHAPTER 12

WILLIAM SELLS THE TWINS

William and Ginger, William's faithful friend and ally, were in a state of bankruptcy. They lacked even the paltry twopence necessary to buy sweets in these days of inflated prices, and life was unendurable. They had approached the adult members of their respective families, only to meet that callousness and indifference so characteristic of adults in their dealings with the young . . .

They sat in the open space of ground behind Ginger's house, and solemnly considered their assets.

Asset 1. – An India-rubber ball with a hole in it, which they had offered to the boy next door for sixpence and which he had refused.

Asset 2. – A pansy root surreptitiously taken from William's father's garden. They had taken this to the local nursery gardener and offered it to him for fivepence-halfpenny. They had afterwards retrieved it from the gutter whither that irascible man had flung it in indignant fury.

Asset 3. – The twins.

The twins *really* belonged to Ginger. That is to say, they were Ginger's cousins and were paying a visit to Ginger's family. They had been there a week now, and to Ginger it had been a very long week. On their arrival, he had found to his horror that he was expected to take an interest in them, even to the extent of taking them about with him wherever he went.

He had almost become accustomed, by now, to their continual presence, but still he disliked them intensely. In all his daring adventures and escapades and games he was to be hampered by the two of them, George and John, both placid, both plump, both three and a half years old. He had to listen to William's comments on their appearance and mental powers, comments with which he privately agreed, but which, for the sake of the honour of his family, he was obliged to resent and avenge . . .

Today, to add insult to injury, his mother had told him to 'see that they kept clean', as their mother was coming to take them home that afternoon. That, at any rate, was a blessing. It would be the last day of his persecution. But the ignominy . . . that a desperate bravado should have to spend his noble energy keeping children clean . . .

George and John were sitting now on the ground, pulling up bits of grass and eating them. William and Ginger watched them scornfully.

'Pity we can't make a bit of money out of them,' said William.

'Umph,' agreed Ginger. 'They've been enough trouble.'

A speculative look came into William's eye.

' 'F we'd lived in historical times,' he said, 'we might have sold them as slaves like wot Miss Jones told us about.'

Ginger gasped at the daring idea. Then his eye fell upon them gloomily.

'No one would have bought 'em,' he said. 'No one wot knew them 's well as I do.'

'You silly!' said William. 'They *wouldn't* know them. They'd just see them in a kind of particular place and think they looked nice—'

'Well, they don't!'

'– or cheap and jus' buy them.'

'Well, wot for? Fancy anyone payin' money for them! . . . For *those*!'

'You're so silly,' said William patiently. 'They'd jus' buy 'em once when they were quite little an' jus pay once for 'em and then have 'em all the rest of their lives to do work for 'em an' they'd never pay any more after they'd jus' paid for 'em once – see?'

Ginger brightened.

'D'you think anyone *would*?' he said.

William replied with superior scorn.

''F you'd been listening in history today you'd know that people don't do it now. Someone or other stopped 'em.'

Ginger considered this deeply.

'You never know,' he said; 'it might be comin' in fashion again. Things do. We might try it. You never know. Someone might jus' like the look of 'em or think 'em cheap or—'

Even William was horrified.

'Yes,' he broke in, 'an' then when you've sold 'em, what'll you say to their mother? . . . Jus' you tell me that! What'll you say to their mother when you've sold 'em?'

Ginger had been considering deeply. Suddenly his brow cleared.

'I know. We could watch where they took 'em to – the ones that bought 'em – an' rescue 'em 'fore anyone knows anything about it.'

'Sounds all right,' said William guardedly.

Ginger turned to his charges.

'You'd like to be slaves, wun't you?' he asked brightly and persuasively.

'*Yiss!*' chorused George and John.

'You see?' said Ginger triumphantly to William. 'I'll go

an' fix things up. 'S worth tryin' anyway.'

'*Sounds* all right,' said William again doubtfully; and added gloomily, out of the vast store of his experience, 'but you never know where things ends.'

A few minutes later Ginger brought two large luggage labels, each inscribed:

> **SLAVE CHEEP**

and on the back of each label was printed:

> **$6\frac{1}{2}$D**

He fastened a label to each twin's neck, to their riotous delight. Then they sat on the open space by the roadside awaiting customers. But it seemed to be a slack time for the slave trade. Only three people passed, and they did not even look at the patient group of four eager small boys.

The procedure had been explained to George and John, as far as their infant intelligences could absorb it, and they expressed themselves willing and anxious to be sold and rescued.

At last, when they were tired of waiting, a fourth

passer-by appeared, an old man, walking very slowly. William, taking his courage in both hands, approached him.

'Do you want a slave?' he asked.

'Eh?' said the old man.

'Do you want a slave?'

'What?' said the old man.

'Do – you – want – a – slave?' repeated William slowly.

'Speak up! Speak up!' said the old man irritably. 'Can't you see I'm deaf? What do you want? What do you want?'

William, whose nerves were suffering from the repetition of the question, cleared his throat and shouted again hoarsely:

'Do – you – want – a – slave?'

The old man snorted.

'Want a shave? Want a shave?' he said angrily. 'No, I *don't* want a shave. You impudent little boy! You little rascal!'

He made a feint at William with his stick, then went off, muttering to himself.

William, slightly shaken by the encounter, returned to his friends.

'It's no good doin' it this way,' he said despondently. 'We shall have to take 'em round to people's houses, like wot they do brushes an' things.'

The twins gave a scream of delight at the suggestion. Then they trotted off happily – George holding Ginger's hand and John William's, both wearing their labels.

'Let's go a good way off,' said Ginger; 'somewhere where they won't know us.'

They walked down a few streets, till William said: 'We'll go into the first house round the corner.' William was looking pale, but resolved. Having embarked upon the dangerous venture, he was determined to carry it through. They came to the next house round the corner, and walked up an overshadowed, neglected drive. They slackened speed considerably as they neared the door.

'You'd better do the talkin',' said Ginger faintly, with a propitiatory air. 'You're better at talkin' than wot I am.'

'Oh, I am, am I?' said William irritably. 'Yes, you think so, *don't* you? Oh, yes, you think so when it's a kind of talkin' you don't want to do! Oh, yes! Huh!'

They stood apprehensively on the front doorstep and gazed at the milk jug that was standing there.

'Looks as if they was out,' said Ginger.

'Oh, yes,' said William, scathing but relieved. 'You don't mind doin' the talkin' now, do you? You don't think I'm better at talkin' than wot you are *now*, do you? You don't mind talkin' to a milk jug. Oh, no!'

'You think you're so clever,' said Ginger bitterly. 'Who

thought of makin' 'em slaves first of all, anyway? Jus' tell me *that*.'

'Well, wot good's it done?' retorted William. 'Nobody'll buy 'em. Takin' 'em to an ole empty house, wot good's *that* done? You tell me *that*!'

The argument would have pursued its normal course to physical violence had not George raised his voice plaintively.

'Wanner be a save,' he pleaded.

With a heroic gesture and lips firmly shut, William raised his hand to the bell and pulled hard. 'That'll show 'em!' he said, darkly. The echoes of the bell died slowly away within the house. No sound of human habitation broke the tense silence on the front doorstep.

'Well,' said William weakly, 'that's *shown* 'em, anyway!'

Then he peered suddenly into the milk jug.

'Crumbs!' he exclaimed. 'A bob!'

Slowly he withdrew the coin, and turned his eyes towards the twins.

'It'll jus' pay for 'em,' he said. 'They're cheap today.'

Ginger was taken aback.

'But – but you don't know they want 'em.'

'Want 'em! Of course they want 'em,' said William scornfully. 'Anyone'd want 'em. Two slaves – cheap at that!

I bet they'd have fetched pounds and pounds in historical times. 'S only 'cause they're a bit out of fashion that they've bin sold at sixpence halfpenny.'

At this moment a milk-boy appeared, staggering up the drive, and William hastily put the coin into his pocket.

' 'Ello, kids!' said the milk-boy.

At other moments William might have made a practical protest against the appellation. But he felt his present position to be too precarious for active aggression. He merely replied coldly:

' 'Ello, Milky!'

'If you belong 'ere,' went on the milk-boy cheerfully, having filled the jug, 'tell 'em they've forgot the money. So long! Be good!'

With a certain relief they watched his figure disappear round the gateway. John at once raised his voice.

'Wanner be a *save*,' he demanded tearfully.

'Wanner be a *save*,' joined in George.

William looked round desperately.

'Here, have a drink of nice milk,' he said.

They obeyed. They fought for the milk jug, and spilt some upon their labels and some upon their coats, but they both managed to drink a fair amount. Finally, they put down the empty jug between them and beamed complacently upon the world again.

'THERE, HAVE A DRINK OF NICE MILK,' SAID WILLIAM. THE
TWINS OBEYED. THEY FOUGHT FOR THE MILK JUG, BUT
BOTH MANAGED TO DRINK A FAIR AMOUNT.

'Let's leave 'em and go an' spend the shilling,' said
William. 'An' then come back an' rescue them.'

'Oh, *yiss*!' said the twins.

William and Ginger went slowly down the drive. At the end they turned round. The twins were sitting side by side on the doorstep, smiling and waving fat hands. Their labels were milky and slightly awry, but still they adhered to their persons. William and Ginger turned into the road. William took out the shilling.

'I say,' said Ginger, 'I – I suppose it's honest?'

'Honest!' said William scornfully. ''S more than honest. We've *give* them a penny. The slaves was sixpence halfpenny each – proper price – an' we've only took a shilling.'

The shilling was successful. It provided them with liquorice, bull's-eyes, two surprise packets, and an India-rubber ball. In their bliss they forgot the flight of time. It was Ginger who remembered it first.

'I say,' he said, 'we'd better be doin' that rescuin' quick. Their mother'll be here soon.'

They set off down the road. Both walked jauntily, as though to hide some secret apprehension.

'Hope we'll be able to rescue them,' said William, with an attempt at lightness.

'Oh, that'll be all right,' said Ginger, with an unconvincing carelessness of tone.

In both their minds was a horrible vision in which the twins' mother played the part of avenging fury.

They walked up the drive. The twins were not on the doorstep. A broken milk jug alone marked the scene of their parting from the twins. Their hearts sank yet farther as they surveyed it.

'Well,' said Ginger, moistening his lips, 'we'd better start rescuin'.'

Drawing a deep breath, he rang the bell. Again the echoes died away in distant regions. Again there came no sounds of human habitation. There was horror on William's freckled face. His naturally wild hair was at its wildest. The vision of the outraged parent of the twins seemed to fill the whole world.

'They're sure to be somewhere,' said Ginger, still with his gallant but ineffectual attempt at lightness.

'Oh, yes!' agreed William gloomily. '*You* can tell her that!'

They searched the garden. They threw stones at the windows. They called: 'Georgie!' and 'Johnnie!' hoarsely, and with a pathetic appeal they had never used to those infants before. Then they turned very slowly towards the gate.

'What can we do now?' said Ginger.

'Nothin',' said William shortly.

Very, very slowly they began to walk down the road.

'You can do the talkin' to their mother,' said William.

'I was goin' to do the talkin' before, wasn't I? Well, *you* can do it now.'

'Oh, yes,' said Ginger, with weary sarcasm. 'A lot of talkin' you did, didn't you? Anyway, there won't need to be much talkin' – not from us! *She'll* do the talkin' all right!'

After a short silence, Ginger spoke again:

'Anyway,' he said in a feeble voice, 'we got a jolly lot of things for that bob!'

It was a feeble remark, and was treated by William with the contemptuous silence it deserved.

As they turned the corner of the road, a lady wearing a tall toque came into sight, walking hurriedly towards them.

'It's her!' said Ginger, with a groan.

'Where are the twins?' she demanded sternly.

To William it seemed as if his heart descended through his boots into the centre of the earth.

'Where are the twins?' she said again.

It was William who answered.

'We don't know,' he said desperately. 'We've sold 'em. We've sold 'em as slaves.'

The twins, left to themselves on the doorstep, replete with excitement and milk, fell happily asleep upon each other's shoulders . . . The minutes passed by.

They awoke to find a young man looking at them in

bewilderment. With him were two ladies, one tall and thin, one short and fat.

'Where do you live, little boys?' said the tall lady.

George smiled at her.

'Here,' he said brightly. 'We're saves.'

The young man raised a hand to his brow.

'Good Lord!' he groaned. 'Surely they don't go with the house – fixtures or something.'

The tall lady was looking at them with a dark frown.

'It's strange,' she said; 'there must be some meaning in it.'

The young man took out a latchkey, stumbled over the milk jug, and entered the hall, followed by the tall lady, the short lady, John and George.

'They can't go with the house,' said the young man plaintively. 'I took it furnished – but, good heavens, furniture *can't* include – these!'

'Did you know the man you took it from?' said the short one.

'No; we fixed everything up by letter, and he cleared out this morning.'

'There's some *meaning* in it if only we knew,' said the tall one again, mysteriously.

'We're saves,' said John. 'Willum comin' soon.'

'Good Lord! Another!' groaned the young man.

' "Slaves 6½d",' she read out. 'It must be a code. They may be a – er – plant, don't you call it? A confidence trick . . . burglar's trap. I think we ought to take them straight to Dr Barnardo's Homes.'

'But perhaps they aren't waifs,' said the stout one. 'Are you waifs, darlings?'

'No; saves,' said George. 'An' William comin' soon.'

'I see it all,' said the stout one suddenly, 'it's as clear as daylight. William's the burglar. He's sent them to help him effect an entrance.'

'Oo, I'm hungry,' said John.

His plaint broke suddenly into a loud howl, in which George joined. Their united efforts produced a noise that made the tall lady lean back against the wall with eyes closed and a hand on her head, and sent the young man flying into the kitchen.

'Where's the larder?' he cried desperately. 'Food! Food at any price! He said he'd get in necessities. Do something . . . anything . . . They'll have fits or something!'

'Oh, I can't bear it,' moaned the tall lady faintly.

The young man came running back with a pot of honey and a pot of jam. He handed one to each of the twins, and the yells subsided. The tall lady opened her eyes, and the young man mopped his brow.

'I can't stand any more of this,' he said. 'I've come here

to work quietly. If they go with the house, I shan't be able to work any way at all.'

'Dear nephew,' said the tall lady, 'we will never desert you.'

'It's awfully good of you, Aunt,' he said hastily. 'But I shouldn't dream of presuming on your kindness. You were only coming to settle me in, you know.'

'Before I go,' she said with firmness, 'I must solve the mystery of these dear children.'

She took up their labels again, and studied them with knitted brows.

'I've come to the definite conclusion,' she said at last, 'that it's a code . . . It's some kind of message.'

'But who from?' said the other.

'Give me time,' she answered with dignity. 'I must decipher the code first.'

They all looked at the twins. George smiled through a thick covering of honey. John smiled through a thick covering of jam. They sat in pools of jam and honey.

'He'll make me pay for that,' said the young man. 'He'll say I'm responsible.'

'You are, dear, legally,' said the stout one brightly. 'Now, I'm going to talk to these dear children, and get to the bottom of this. Now, darlings, who's William?'

'Willum's nice!' said George.

'Yes, darling, but what does he do? Who is he?'

'Willum sells us!' said John proudly.

'He doesn't sell little boys, surely?' said the tall lady, aghast.

George and John nodded their heads.

'Yiss, he does.'

'He's not your father, is he?'

'Oh, no,' they chorused. 'He's Willum. He sells us.'

'A kidnapper!' said the stout lady sharply. 'That's it. A kidnapper! We must get to the bottom of this. We must confront the man . . .'

'I still think,' said the other dreamily, 'that it's a – plant – or a code.'

'Do you know where William lives?' asked the stout lady of George.

'Oh, yiss!' said George proudly.

'I will confront this man,' she said dramatically, 'and you must support me.'

The young man groaned.

'It's all like a nightmare,' he said. 'It'll knock me off work for months.'

'Couldn't you use it?' suggested the stout lady. 'It would make a most sensational plot . . . the mysterious children . . . the code . . . the—'

'Thank you,' said the young man coldly, 'I don't go in for sensational plots.'

The procession set out – first, John and the stout lady, then George and the thin lady, then the young man, wearing a set agonised expression.

'And I came here for quiet and rest,' he muttered pathetically.

'Take us to William's house, darling,' said the stout lady to John.

'We ought to have brought some sort of a weapon,' said her sister grimly.

'Vivian will protect us,' said the other bravely.

Vivian groaned again in the gathering dusk.

The twins had led the procession on to the common with every sign of confidence, but now they stopped.

'Want more *dam*,' said John.

'Wanner go *home*,' said George.

'We'll just go down this path and see if it leads anywhere,' said the short lady uncertainly. 'Vivian will stay with the children.'

They returned in a few minutes.

'Nothing to be seen – absolutely nothing. It's most unfortunate. Vivian, where are the children?'

Vivian, who was leaning against a tree, his eyes dreamily fixed on the distance, roused himself.

'What children? . . . Oh, damn! I'd forgotten them . . . Here, aren't they? Just messing about . . . they were . . . I'd just got an idea when you disturbed me.'

'But the children?' gasped the stout one, staring wildly round the dim landscape. The young man ran his fingers through his hair. The thin lady gave a little scream.

'It was all a plot. They've led us to a lonely spot, and now someone's going to murder us.'

'They'll be all right,' said the young man, miserably. 'Children always are. I'm getting a cold. Let's go home.'

'Don't be foolish,' said the stout one sternly. 'I will not move from this spot till I have found the children. If necessary I will search all night and you with me.'

They began to trudge wearily in single file along the narrow path.

'Oo, someone's coming,' screamed the thin lady. 'Let us be brave . . . Offer no resistance . . . They're sure to be desperate . . . Vivian, for my sake, don't be rash . . . Don't kill anyone.'

But it was another little procession that was approaching them, as weary-looking as their own. At the head walked a woman in a tall toque. At the end walked a small boy with freckles and untidy hair and a dejected expression. They peered into each other's faces.

'Have you seen two little boys?' they all began simultaneously.

'John,' said the twins' mother.

'George,' said the stout lady.

Then the thin lady and the twins' mother had hysterics.

It was William who found them in a dry ditch near by. They were fast asleep, with blissful smiles upon their mouths, besmeared with jam and honey. They awoke and stared in amazement at the crowd of friends and relations.

'Nice William!' murmured George sleepily.

'Wanner be a save adain,' said John. 'Want more dam!'

CHAPTER 13

WILLIAM'S HELPING HAND

William was on his way to visit his new friend. He whistled as he went, his lips pursed determinedly, his brows drawn into a scowl of absorption, his untidy hair standing, like a somewhat unsaintly halo, round his head. When William whistled, he could be heard a long way off. It was an affair of great effort and concentration. It was a sound before which strong men quailed.

William's new friend heard the sound long before William had turned the corner that led to his house. He put his hand to his head and groaned.

William's new friend was Vivian Strange, the distinguished poet and journalist. Vivian Strange had taken a furnished house in the village in order to enjoy the calm and quiet which were so essential to his literary calling. Instead of calm and quiet he had found William. That is, William had adopted him.

William was attracted to Vivian Strange because, although Vivian Strange belonged to the tyrant race of the 'grown-ups' he had never yet told William to wipe his boots or go home at once or not to speak till he was spoken to. This touched William deeply. He was not used to it. He imagined that it must hide a lasting affection for him on the part of Strange. As a matter of fact it did no such thing. The attitude of Vivian Strange to William may be compared to that of a timid fawn before a lion, or a rabbit before a snake. He was not used to the human boy. He had never known one before at close quarters. When he gently hinted to William that he must be missed at home, William kindly intimated that they didn't mind a bit and he could stay a good long time yet.

Such mild sarcasm as Strange could produce had the same effect on William as water on the back of the proverbial duck. William was not used to hints. William was not used either to houses where he could sit in the best chairs and talk to his heart's content and eat cake unrestrained. He made the most of it. He liked Vivian Strange.

And Vivian told himself bitterly every night that his genius was being ruined, his naturally sweet temper embittered, his constitution undermined by a creature less than half his own size whom he might almost kill with one hand. He often dreamed of William. He often recalled hard things he had read or heard about the human boy, and decided that they were all true. Yet, when he met William's mother, and William's mother said, 'I do hope that William isn't a nuisance to you,' he flushed and said hastily, 'Oh, no, not at all. I like it.' And William's mother went placidly on her way and remarked later to an incredulous family circle, 'There must be *something* about William for a brilliant literary man like Mr Strange to take pleasure in his company.' Thereupon the family raised incredulous eyebrows.

On the previous day William had paid three visits to his new friend. The first visit had nipped in the bud a very promising poem written in an uncommon metre.

William entered playing on his mouth organ a tune that he had learnt (not quite correctly, he admitted) that morning. During the third repetition of the tune, Vivian Strange began to see red, but his curse of politeness still clung to him.

'Hadn't you better let them hear that at home?' he said desperately.

William wiped his mouth politely.

'Oh, no,' he said. 'I don't mind goin' on a bit longer. 'Sides my family's not as fond of musick as wot you are.'

When William had gone, Strange returned to the poem, but inspiration had fled.

After lunch he began a strikingly original essay on 'Nature the Divine'. Then William called again. This time he proudly brought a live mouse and a dead hedgehog to show his friend. He also carried (with difficulty) a jar full of muddy water containing squirming water creatures of repellent appearance and sinister expressions.

Vivian Strange pricked his finger on the dead hedgehog and was bitten by the mouse. On retiring precipitately from the mouse he knocked over the jar of water which William had thoughtfully placed on the edge of his bureau. Holding his bitten finger in his mouth, he watched the water as it dripped partly on the carpet, partly upon a new satin cushion. He also watched his blotting-paper and pens and stamps and literary master-pieces floating in mud amongst wriggling, nightmare creatures. He raised his hand to his head.

'This,' he said, 'is the last straw.'

William, who was on his knees, rescuing as many of the creatures as he could, raised a face purple with effort.

''S all right,' he said pleasantly. 'Don't you worry about it. I don't mind. Honest, I don't. I can get some more. Honest, I can . . . an' anyway, some's not dead. You didn't reely get a proper look at 'em, did you? I'll get some more tomorrow an' you can have 'em to keep. But don't you worry about droppin' 'em. I don't mind.'

Half an hour later, his face pale and set, Vivian took up his half-written essay, 'Nature the Divine'. There was a muddy pool through the middle of it, and a tadpole's corpse reposed peacefully in one corner. With averted eyes Vivian dropped it into the fire.

As he lay wakeful through the night, he searched in his mind for some form of literature that could resist the blighting effects of his young friend's frequent and devastating visits. With a lightning flash of inspiration came the answer – a sensational story. Vivian had never before lowered his genius to writing a sensational story, but he felt that the time had come. Some story that would carry itself along of its own momentum, that even a visit from William would not be able to turn from its course.

He was deep in the throes of it the next afternoon when the shrill sound of William's distant whistle reached him.

William entered cheerfully.

'Hello,' he said. 'You writin'?'

The victim raised his face from his hands.

'I *was*,' he said pointedly.

'I thought you was,' said William. 'I saw you through the window with your head in your hands, like as if you couldn't think wot to write nex'. So I knew you'd be glad to see me.'

As he spoke, his rare smile overspread his freckled face.

The young man was dumb.

'I used to write a bit myself,' went on William modestly,

'an' often I couldn't think wot to write nex'. I remember once I wrote an orfully good tale about a man wot was a pirate an' he was run after by a dastardly cannibal round an' round a desert island an' then the dastardly cannibal caught him an' was jus' goin' to cook him when some frens of the dastardly cannibal came up, an' while the dastardly cannibal was saying "good afternoon" to them the pirate got up a tree an' waved his pocket handkerchief to another pirate wot was on the sea as a sign that he was in deadly danger.'

William stopped. 'Yes?' said his unfortunate hearer in a dull voice. William plunged on.

'An' the dastardly cannibal sawed down the tree but the other pirate came an' they escaped an' the proud an' beautiful daughter of the dastardly cannibal escaped with them. She wasn't dastardly like wot her father was. She didn't like eatin' human folks. She didn't like the taste, so she was glad to get to a country where they didn't do it an' they was married an' she was the queen of the pirates an' he was the king of the pirates, an' she was proud an' beautiful an' said 'Avaunt!' when anyone tried to cheek her jus' like a reel queen. Is your tale anything like that?'

'No,' groaned Mr Strange.

'Well,' said William, comfortably ensconced in an armchair, 'now I've told you my tale, you oughter tell me yours. I say, is there any of that cake left wot you so kin'ly gave me some of yesterday?'

The young man waved a limp hand towards the sideboard cupboard.

William took a large slice of plum cake and returned to his chair.

'I always get so's I mus' have something to eat about this time, don't you?' he said pleasantly. 'I *can* eat mos' times but sometimes I feel so's I *mus'* eat . . . Well, go on an' tell me about your tale, now. I've told you about mine an' I'll help you, you know, about wot to write nex'.'

'I don't want you to,' said the young man desperately.

'Oh, it's no bother,' said William, kindly. 'Don't you think about that. I wanter help you. You gave me big bits of cake today an' yesterday an' I wanter help you an' I've wrote tales myself an' I know wot it's like. An' don't worry about knockin' over my water things. I've gotter fren who's promised to catch some more tomorrow an' we'll bring them along soon's we've gottem. That was jolly good cake.' The young man automatically waved a hand towards the cupboard again.

'Thanks. I don't mind a bit more. It's *jolly* good cake . . . Now tell me about your tale so's I can help. Wot's it about?'

'It's – it's just about a man,' said Mr Strange feebly.

'Wot sort of a man?' said William with his mouth full of cake.

'Just a man – he's going home one night—'

'Goin' home, where from?' demanded William.

'That doesn't come into the story,' said the young man irritably. 'He was just going home.'

'All right,' said William soothingly. 'Only, if he was goin' home he must 'a' been somewhere, an' I jus' wondered where he'd been to be coming home from.'

'Well, as he's coming home he gets a message that a girl – a girl—' the young man hesitated.

'The girl wot he's in love with?' supplied William earnestly.

'Er – yes,' said the young man. 'He gets a message that she's in danger and he must go to her at once, so he follows the man, you see—'

'Which follows which?' said William judicially.

'The man the story begins with—'

'The one wot you didn't know where he was goin' home from?'

'Yes. That. Well, he follows the man that tells him the girl's in danger and really the man—'

'If you don't call 'em names,' said William, 'I can't tell which is which. Let's call the man wot you don't know where he was goin' home from Alberto (that's a good tale name), and the one wot says that the girl wot Alberto's in love with's in deadly danger Rudolpho (they all end with -o in a book I've been readin'; it sounded fine). Well then, Rudolpho tells Alberto that the girl wot Alberto's in love with's in deadly danger. I think that's a jolly good tale, but I think that Alberto oughter have a secret treasure somewhere, an' let's have another man in called Archibaldo (I've gotter nuncle called Archibald) wot wants the secret treasure an' he's gotter trail of dynamite laid to right under Alberto's bed to blow him up in the night when's he's asleep, an' let's have another girl in called Rosabellina wot Rudolpho's in love with – a proud an' beautiful maiden, you know, an' Rudolpho gets hold of her an' she yells out, "Avaunt! Unhand me, varlet! . . ." Well, you finish yours first an' we'll put in my bits afterwards. You'd jus' got to Alberto comin' home from somewhere you din't know where an' followin' Rudolpho . . . Wot comes next?'

Vivian Strange stared in front of him. He was once more the rabbit and William the snake. Some power in William's earnest, freckled countenance compelled him to proceed.

'The – er – the second man was really a secret service agent—'

'Wot's that?' inquired William disapprovingly.

'Oh, it's – er – it's a kind of glorified policeman, I suppose.'

'Much better have him a pirate or a red injun,' said William, 'but never mind. Go on.'

'Well, he wants to get hold of some letters that – er – Alberto has, and leads him to a lonely house and locks him up there, and says he'll keep him there till he gives them up.'

'Hurlin' vile threats?' said William, his face alight with earnestness. 'Let him say it hurlin' vile threats an' precautions an' insults in his teeth. Wot happens nex'?'

'I don't know,' said the young man. 'That's as far as I got. I can't get on with it. I can't think what he'd say or do next.'

William drew his brows together in deep thought.

'I should think Alberto oughter say "Ha! Villain! Never shalt thou worst me" – or something like that.'

'People don't talk like that in real life.'

'Oh, reel life!' said William scornfully. 'I thought we was talkin' about books.'

'Don't you think your friends want you to play with them?' said Mr Strange with emphasis. 'Don't you think you've left them for quite long enough?'

William arose and brushed the cake crumbs from his coat to the carpet.

'P'raps I'd better be goin',' he agreed. 'But I'll be thinkin' over wot comes nex'. You say you want it real life an' not books. I think you oughter have more people in it. Can't you have them all on a desert island an' make Rudolpho get eaten by cannibals in mistake for Alberto? . . . Oh, well, jus' as you like, of course. I'll bring you my tales to read one day an' I'll bring you some water things tomorrow. Did you know tadpoles ate tadpoles? Talk about cannibals! . . . I say, that's a jolly fine penknife.'

Vivian Strange, whose proud spirit was broken, handed him the knife with a despairing gesture.

'Take it!' he moaned. 'Take it and go!'

William was touched.

'Oh, no,' he said. 'I'd better not take such a jolly fine penknife as that. You're sure to be wantin' it again. But – but I'll borrow it for a bit if you don't mind. I'll bring it back when I bring the water animals. I say, it's jolly kind of you. Well, goodbye.'

William closed the door behind him. The sudden peace and silence of the room seemed to Strange too blissful to be real. But the door opened and William's tousled head and earnest face appeared again.

'I say,' he said. 'How about having a burglar in an' a detective after him, you know, an' mysterious signs an' clues an' bloodhounds – as well as the other people? . . .

Not? . . .Well, it's your tale, so you jus' do it how you like.
I'll see you again soon. Well, goodbye.'

William disappeared and the front door opened and
shut. With anxious eyes Vivian Strange watched through
the window for William's youthful form to appear in the
drive leading to the gate. It did not do so. Instead, the
familiar untidy head appeared once more round the door.

'I say!' he said. 'I was jus' tryin' to remember – did I
have three pieces of cake in here, or only two? . . . Oh,
thanks . . . I say, it's jolly kind of you.'

'Take it all,' said Mr Strange, 'and go!'

William was still more touched.

'Oh, no!' he said as he opened the cupboard. 'I won't
take it all – not jus' now. I'll take one more piece now an'
I'll come round for another piece later on. It gets so
messed up carryin' it about in your pockets, cake does. I've
tried it. Gets all mixed up with marbles an' bits of clay an'
string an' things. It doesn't spoil the taste but it wastes it
– gettin' it all crumby . . .Well, goodbye.'

Once more the front door opened and shut. Once
more there was silence and peace. Vivian Strange, with a
deep sigh, stretched out for his pen. Then an expression of
wild despair came over his face . . . The well-known footsteps sounded in the hall again and the door opened.

'I nearly went away,' said William affectionately, 'without showin' you my new whistle. I've been practisin' an' practisin' so's to show it you this afternoon. An' I nearly forgot an' I'd have had to come all the way back. This is it.'

He placed two fingers in the corners of his mouth and emitted a siren-like sound that caused his friend to leap suddenly into the air in terror and surprise. William smiled with pride and friendliness.

'I knew you'd like it,' he said. 'My family doesn't care for it at home, but they don't care for any whistles. They don't reely like musick – not like you do. Well, goodbye.'

William walked along the road, humming happily to himself. His humming was, if possible, more dreadful than his whistling. William only hummed when he was happy. He enjoyed the sound of his humming. In this he was absolutely unique . . .

He was extremely happy today. His heart warmed at the thought of his friend's kindness . . . the confidential literary chat . . . the cake . . . the penknife . . . He took out the knife and looked at it. His heart swelled with pride and pleasure . . . a knife like that . . . and he'd been ready to give it . . . *give* it . . . it was jolly decent of him . . . William had no other friend in the whole world who would have thought of *lending* him a knife like that, much less *giving* it.

William's sense of gratitude was not easily stirred, but it was stirred this afternoon. When stirred, it demanded immediate and practical expression . . . He must *do* something for his friend . . . now . . . at once . . . But what? . . . He could get him the water things, of course, but that wasn't enough. What did Mr Strange really *want*? . . . Suddenly William's sombre countenance lit up . . . He'd wanted to know what Alberto would have said and done in real life . . . He should know.

Mr Porter was walking home. Mr Porter was an eminently respectable gentleman who lived a quiet, hard-working life divided between an eminently respectable office and an eminently respectable home. Mr Porter was on his way home from the station, carrying his attaché case in his hand as he had done for the last thirty years.

In his mind was a pleasurable anticipation of a warm fire, comfortable bedroom slippers, a well-cooked dinner, a glass of good wine, an excellent cigar, and the evening paper. Mr Porter had walked home with this pleasurable anticipation in his mind for the last thirty years, and it had always been fulfilled. There was a rosy glow over all his thoughts. He hardly noticed the small boy with the freckled, scowling countenance till he actually addressed him.

'The lady wot you're in love with,' said the boy to him

suddenly in an expressionless tone, 'is in deadly danger, an' says you're to go to her at once.'

Mr Porter stopped short and peered through the dusk. He felt a little frightened. 'The lady wot—' he repeated. Then, 'Would you mind sayin it again?'

William didn't mind.

'The lady wot you're in love with,' he said clearly and distinctly, 'is in deadly danger an' says you're to go to her at once.'

'The lady wot—' began Mr Porter again. 'What a curious expression! Do you – er – do you mean my wife?'

'I s'pose so,' said William guardedly.

'Er – did she tell you to say that?'

'Yes.'

'Was she a tall lady?'

'Yes,' said William, taking the line of least resistance.

'With a mole on her left cheek?'

'Yes.'

'Grey hair?'

'Yes.'

'*Most* curious!' said Mr Porter. 'That's certainly my wife. What did you say she said?'

'The lady wot you're in love with,' said William monotonously, 'is in deadly danger, an' says you're to go to her at once.'

'But – where is she?'

'She said you was to follow me.'

'Most curious!' said Mr Porter uncertainly. '*Most* curious! Well – er – I suppose I'd better – er – one never knows – is it far?'

William's eye gleamed with victory.

'Oh, no,' he said soothingly, 'not far.'

But Mr Porter's heart had sunk. The rosy vision of the warm fire, the comfortable bedroom slippers, well-cooked dinner, glass of wine, cigar, evening paper seemed to have retreated to an incalculable distance.

'Be as quick as you can,' he said irritably. 'I can't stand here all night catching my death of cold. How do I know it's not some cock-and-bull story? Hurry up! Hurry up!'

Silently and happily William led the way. Silently and miserably Mr Porter followed. Mr Porter disliked above all things departing a hair's breadth from his usual routine. What *was* it all about, anyway? What was Mary thinking of, sending that curious message? Who was this strange boy? His self-pity and righteous indignation increased at every step. Down the street . . . round a corner . . . in at a side-gate . . . down a side-path past a house . . . into a back garden . . . What the—? The strange boy was holding open the door of a kind of outhouse.

'THE LADY WOT YOU'RE IN LOVE WITH,' SAID WILLIAM,
'IS IN DEADLY DANGER, AN' SAYS YOU'RE TO GO TO HER
AT ONCE.'

'She said particular you was to go in here,' said the boy simply.

'What the—?' blazed Mr Porter. 'What the—?' he sputtered again.

The boy looked at him dispassionately.

'She said particular you was to go in here.'

'Into a—? Into a dirty, empty coal-shed? What—?'

Mr Porter stepped into the outhouse and flashed his electric torch around it. In that second he satisfied himself that the shed was empty. In that second also the door banged to behind him and a key was turned in the lock.

'Here!' cried Mr Porter angrily. 'Where the—?'

There was no answer.

Mr Porter banged ferociously at the door.

'Open the door, you young villain!' he shouted.

There was no answer.

Mr Porter kicked the door, and shook the door, and rattled the door, and cursed the door. The door remained immovable, and only the silence answered him. Having recourse once more to his electric torch, he discovered a small window high up at the back of the shed and beneath it a pile of coal. Mr Porter determined to reach the window over the coal. He climbed the coal, and slipped in the coal, and waded in the coal, and rolled in the coal, and wallowed in the coal, and lost his collar in the coal.

Finally he let fly a torrent of language whose eloquence, and variety, and emphasis, and richness surprised even himself. Mr Porter, an hour ago, would have believed himself incapable of such language. Then, panting, covered with coal dust, his collar gone, his coat torn, he surveyed the scene of his imprisonment, and there came to him a vision of a warm fire, comfortable bedroom slippers, a well-cooked dinner, a glass of wine, a good cigar and the evening paper . . . In sudden frenzy he flung himself bodily upon the door.

Vivian Strange had given up all attempt to write. He was sitting in the armchair by the fire reading poetry to soothe his nerves. His nerves were very much upset. He kept imagining that he heard strange noises – bangs and shouts, and once he shuddered, imagining that he heard William's whistle. He decided to go back to town as soon as possible. The much vaunted peace of the countryside was a fiction. The country was not peaceful. It contained William, and William's whistle, and William's water creatures, and William's conversations. There was more peace in the middle of Piccadilly – without William – than there was in the country with William.

The door opened suddenly and William appeared.

There was on his face, a look of conscious pride as of one who has something attempted something done, but is prepared to be quite modest about it.

'You can go an' hear wot he says an' does in reel life,' he said. 'He's sayin' an' doin' it now in the coal-shed. I've been listenin' for ever so long.'

Mr Strange rose wildly.

'But—' he began.

The curious sounds increased. They were real, not a delusion of his overwrought nerves, as he had supposed. William was real too.

'Where—?' he said still more wildly.

'In the coal-shed,' said William impatiently. 'Hurry up or he'll be gettin' tired an' stoppin'. Take some paper an' then you can copy down some of the things he says in reel life. I told you I was right.'

There came a sudden crashing and rending of wood, the sound of angry steps on the gravel, and in front of the house appeared a nightmare figure, black, gesticulating, ragged, collarless, hatless. It was the eminently respectable Mr Porter. 'Police', and 'pay for this', and 'scoundrel', were among the words that reached the bewildered Mr Strange through the window. Then, shaking its fist, the figure disappeared into the dusk.

'There,' said William. 'You're too late. He's got out.

He's broke the door down an' got out. Anyway, you know now wot he does in reel life. He breaks the door down an' gets out. An' I can remember lots of the things he said. I listened quite a long time. I'll take another piece of that cake now, if you don't mind. You said I could. Thanks awfully. I took a lot of trouble gettin' that reel life thing for you. Could – could I keep that penknife jus' for another day? I've got some frens I'd like to show it to. An' if there's anything else you'd like me to find out in reel life, I'll try. I don't bother with reel life myself when I do tales, but if you . . . Oh, I say, are you goin' on with the tale now?'

Mr Strange was not. He was writing a telegram form. It ran:

'Secure berth on any boat sailing anywhere. Complete nervous prostration. Change and rest urgent.'

'I 'speck I'd better go,' said William regretfully. 'It's after my supper-time. You don't mind, do you?'

'No,' said the young man wildly. 'No, I don't mind. I'm going away myself tomorrow, going away for good.'

'Oh, are you?' said William sadly. 'I'm sorry. I shall miss you quite a lot an' I 'speck you'll miss me.'

'Oh, yes,' answered Mr Strange. 'I shall miss you. I hope I shall miss you.'

'Well, don't worry about it,' said William kindly. 'I

'speck you'll be comin' back soon. Goodbye, an' you can get on with your tale now, can't you, now you know wot he says an' does in reel life? Well, goodbye.'

He went briskly out of the front door.

Mr Strange drew a deep, quivering breath of relief. But not for long. Two apparitions appeared before the window, coming up the drive, one the blackened and battered remains of Mr Porter and the other a stalwart arm of the law, carrying a notebook.

There was a gleam in Mr Porter's eye. He was going to execute justice but, justice executed, there lay before him the warm fire, and comfortable bedroom slippers, and well-cooked dinner, and glass of wine, and excellent cigar, and evening paper of his dreams.

But Vivian's horrified gaze was drawn from them by the near vision of William's face pressed against the glass.

'I say,' called William. 'You *did* say I could keep that knife for a bit, didn't you?'

Vivian Strange made a wild gesture that might have been assent or dissent or mere frenzy.

'Thanks awfully,' shouted William. 'Well, goodbye.'

William strolled home through the dusk. He was sorry his friend was going, but, after all, he would be able to keep all the water creatures himself. Giving away water creatures was always a great sacrifice to William. Anyway, he'd had quite a decent day . . . all about that tale had been interesting and exciting, and that was a jolly good cake and a *jolly* good penknife and – his thoughts flew to that thrilling five minutes spent in rapt silence outside the coal-house – he'd learnt a lot of new words.

CHAPTER 14

WILLIAM GETS WRECKED

William laid aside *Robinson Crusoe* with a sigh. His dreams of pirate-king and robber-chief vanished. The desire of his heart now was to be shipwrecked on a desert island. He surveyed his garden and the next garden and the fields beyond with an impatient scowl. He felt bitterly that it was just his luck to live in an overpopulated world with ready-made houses and where everything one could possibly need could be purchased at the shop round the corner . . .

Yet he felt that within reach there must be a desert island, or at any rate some spot which a very little imagination could transform into a desert island. He decided to set out on a voyage. He filled his pockets with biscuits and pieces of string. String was always useful.

He went into the morning-room where his mother and grown-up sister sat. He felt strongly that a mariner just about to be shipwrecked ought to bid a fond farewell to his family.

'Goodbye,' he said in a deep voice, 'case I'm not back.'

'I wish you'd remember to wipe your boots when you come into the house,' said his mother patiently.

'You'd better be back if you want any tea,' said Ethel.

William felt that they lacked every quality that the family of a shipwrecked mariner should possess. Not for the first time he washed his hands of them in disgust.

'All right,' he said. 'Don't blame me if – if you're sorry when it's too late.'

With this cryptic remark he left them.

To a casual observer William looked only a small boy walking slowly down a road, frowning, with his hands in his pockets. He was really an intrepid mariner sailing across an uncharted sea.

'Hello, William.'

William had a weak spot in his heart for Joan. He rather liked her dimples and dark curls. In his softer moments he had contemplated Joan actually reigning by his side as pirate-queen or robber-chieftainess. Now he felt that her presence might enliven a somewhat lonely voyage.

'I'm an explorer,' he said, 'sailin' along an' lookin' for new lands.'

'Oh, William,' Joan pleaded, 'may I come with you?'

He considered the matter with a judicial frown.

'All right,' he said at last. 'Will you come in my ship or

will you have a ship of your own?'

'I'd rather come in your ship, please.'

'All right,' he said. 'Well, you're *in* my ship. Come on.'

She walked along by his side. The best part of Joan was that she asked very few questions.

'We're probably goin' to come to a desert island soon,' said William. 'I *speck* we shall come to a desert island soon if we get through these icebergs all right. There's a pretty awful wind blowin', isn't there – lashin' the sails an' tackin' an' all that an' no land in sight an' all these whales an' things all about?'

'Yes, William,' said Joan obediently.

'You'd better be chief mate,' William advised. 'I'll be skipper. You don't see any land in sight, do you, mate?'

Joan gazed at the road before them, the hedges around them, the cow's head above the hedge, and the figure of the Vicar in the distance.

'No, Will— I mean skipper,' she said.

William heaved a sigh of relief. For a minute he had thought she was going to fail him.

They proceeded in silence for a time.

'The mast's gone now,' said William, 'all crashin' down on the deck before the terrible hurricane wot sweeps all before it. I thought it was goin' to crash on your brave head, mate.'

'Yes, Will— I mean skipper,' said Joan.

She was quite satisfactory. She entered into the spirit of a thing and had the additional advantage of not demanding a prominent role.

The Vicar had come up to them. He looked at William with disapproval.

'Fine day, young man,' he said breezily.

'Awful,' said William gruffly, 'blowin' an' hurricanin' an' lashin' at everything. Come on, mate.'

They left the Vicar staring after them.

'I wonder,' he said to the landscape, 'whether that boy is deficient or merely impudent?'

He was still wondering when they vanished from sight. They reached the river.

'The waves is lashin' up at us,' said William, surveying the placid stream. 'I don't think this ole boat will stick together much longer if we don' see a bit of land soon. I'm jus' drenched through – spite of my tauparlings – an' almost perishin' of hunger 'cause the provisions was swep' overboard, aren't you, mate?'

'Yes, Will— I mean skipper,' said Joan, raising blue eyes alight with admiration.

The path now turned inland. This part of the river was private, and the back garden of a large house swept down to the river's bank.

'I b'lieve – I *b'lieve*,' said William, 'that I see an island – I *b'lieve* that at last I see an island jus' as this ole boat is goin' to crash to pieces against a towerin' rock. *There!* It's crashed to pieces against a towering rock. My goodness! We're in the icy water now! Well, you catch hold of an ole splinter or somethin' an' I'll catch hold of somethin' else, an' we'll jus' make for that ole island with all our might an' main – spite of the rain an' wind lashin' at our faces—'

With set, grim expression he began to struggle through the garden hedge.

'Come on, mate,' he called, holding the bushes aside for her, 'here's the island at last. Now we'll lie down on the sand an' sleep an' then I'll go an' get the things wot will be washed up from the wreck.'

The part of the garden where they found themselves was out of sight of the house. There was a summer house by the river and near that a clothes line with a tablecloth hung out to dry.

They sat down on the bank of the river.

'Nice to rest, isn't it,' said William, 'after all that strugglin' against the fierce wind an' rain?'

'Yes, Will— I mean skipper.'

'You go on restin',' said William, kindly, 'an' I'll go an' try to find things washed up by the wreck.'

*

He crept towards the back of the house. There was no one to be seen. The door stood slightly ajar. Cautiously William peered within. He saw a comfortable kitchen, empty save for the presence of a grey cat washing its face on the hearthrug. It suspended operations for a moment, surveyed William coldly and disapprovingly, and then returned to its ablutions.

William's glance fell eagerly on a box of matches on the table and a saucepan in the sink. He waited in the shadow of the doorway. There was no sound in the house. At last, on tiptoe, his brows drawn together, his tongue projecting from his mouth, his eye fixed on the door, his freckled countenance purple and scowling, his hair standing on end, he crept across the room. Returning the cat's haughty stare, he seized the matches, the saucepan and two cups, and fled down to the river, where his chief mate was sitting on the grass, idly throwing stones into the water.

'Look what I've found washed up from the wreck,' he said proudly. 'Now we'll build a fire an' soon I expect we'll find a native savage an' some wild animals.'

'Not – not *too* wild, William,' said the chief mate.

'All right,' said the skipper, 'not too wild, but anyway it doesn't matter 'cause you've got me an' there's nothing much I can't kill. Now, after the night on the open sea, we'd better make breakfast.' With indescribable joy they collected twigs, made a fire, filled the saucepan with water from the river, and put it on to boil. When the water was warm, William poured it into two cups and broke his biscuits into them. The water was smoked and the biscuits grimy from their sojourn in William's pockets, but to the shipwrecked mariners the draught was as of nectar and ambrosia. Both drained their cups.

'That was grand, wasn't it, mate? I think you oughter say, "Aye, aye, sir."'

'Aye, aye, sir.'

'Well, now, I'd better build us a house out of logs an' things, an' you go and see if you can find anything washed up from the wreck.'

'Oh, William – I mean skipper!'

'You won't mind – there's no one there but a cat.'

With mingled apprehension and excitement, Joan stole off to the house.

William, left alone, turned to the summer house, and in his imagination made it vanish into thin air. Then he went through a ferocious and strenuous pantomime of cutting down trees and piling up logs, and finally beheld the completed summer house with the proud eyes of a creator. Then he opened the door and entered.

A ragged, unkempt man rose from the seat rubbing his

eyes. A black bag was on the floor.

William and the man stared at each other, neither of them flinching.

'You're jus' wot I wanted to find,' said William at last with excitement and friendliness in his voice; 'I jus' wanted a native savage.'

'Oh, yer did, did yer?' said the man. 'Glad I'll do fer yer arl right. An' 'oo may you be if I may be so bold as to arsk?'

'We're shipwrecked,' said William, 'shipwrecked on a desert island. I've jus' built a hut, an' my chief mate's gone to find things washed up from the wreck, an' you'll do for the native savage. Do you mind bein' called Friday?'

'Not at all, young gent,' said the man, 'not at all. 'Erbert 'Ammond is my name, but call me Friday, Saturday *an'* Sunday, if so you've a mind.' (He ran his eye speculatively over William.) 'But it seems funny to see a shipwrecked sailor in clothes like them. You'd 'ave thought they'd 'ave all got tore to pieces in the wreck, like.'

'Yes,' said William eagerly, 'they did.'

'One would 'ave expected to see you – well, p'raps dressed in a sail or something.' His eyes narrowed, and he pointed to the ragged tablecloth fluttering in the breeze. 'That 'ud do fine for a sail.'

William's eyes were alight with enthusiasm.

'Yes – it *would*,' he said, 'fine.'

'If I was you an' bein' shipwrecked,' said the man, deftly taking the tablecloth from the line, 'I'd nip into that there summer house, an' take off that ordinary-like suit an' rig up myself in this here sail . . . then you'd feel like as if you *was* shipwrecked, eh?'

He threw the tablecloth into the summer house, and William, all excitement, followed. Friday lay on the bank by the river, smoked a foul pipe and winked at the landscape.

Soon William emerged proudly wearing the tablecloth in the fashion of a Roman toga.

'That,' said Friday, 'looks a bit of orl *right* – if I was you I'd go an' show it to the hother one wots lookin' at the wreck. I'll stay an' look hafter that there suit of yours so's no one runs off with it.'

As William swaggered slowly towards the house, Friday rose, spat into the river, winked at the tree and went into the summer house again.

Joan was sitting on the step of the house with the cat on her knee.

'Will— I mean skipper,' she said, 'it's a lovely pussy.' Then, 'Oh, goodness – *William*!'

Her tone hovered between horror and admiration.

William stepped jauntily up to her. One corner of the tablecloth trailed on the ground behind him.

'It's a sail,' he said, proudly. 'I got all my clothes dashed off me in the wreck, an' I'm wearing a sail wot got washed up by the waves. It does jolly well, doesn't it?'

Joan clapped her hands.

'Oh, an' I've found a native savage,' went on William, 'an' he doesn't mind bein' called Friday—'

'Oh, how *lovely*! An' the pussy will do for a native wild animal. Oh, *William* – we've got simply *everything*, haven't we?'

They went happily down to the river.

There William sustained the first shock of that momentous afternoon. Many more were to follow. The native savage had disappeared. Search in the summer house revealed the fact that William's clothes had also disappeared.

William's jaw dropped.

'*Stole* 'em!' he ejaculated.

Joan's eyes opened wide. The possibilities of the situation were beginning to dawn on both of them.

'*William* – how'll you get home?'

William's expression was one of pure horror.

'Mean ole *thing*!' he said. 'Simply *stole* 'em.'

'*William* – what'll your mother say?'

They stared at each other in consternation. William clutched the tablecloth tightly round his neck.

At this moment a loud, angry voice came from the house. They fled precipitately to the summer house. Isolated phrases reached them.

'Careless girl . . . gossiping in the grocer's shop . . . *anyone* might have come in . . . not even locked the back door . . . Heaven knows—'

Then they heard the violent slamming of the back door. Both felt that the time had come for the adventure to end. The desert island had lost its charm. It must be after tea-time. The sun was already setting. In normal circumstances, they would have crept quietly from the garden and returned to their respective homes. But circumstances were not normal. Between William's pants and vest and the world at large was – not his usual long-suffering cloth suit – but a trailing and in certain places inadequate tablecloth. William's freckled face, with its expression of indignant horror, in its frame of wild, carroty hair, had a curious, unexpected appearance at the top of the long white robe.

'Oh, let's go home,' said Joan, with a suspicion of tears in her voice.

William looked at her desperately.

'I can't go home like *this*,' he said, hoarse with emotion. 'I can't go through the village wearin' a tablecloth. Everybody'd be laughing at me. No one's ever done it before – not walked through the village in a tablecloth – it'd make me ridic'l'us for the rest of my life.'

He sat down, staring despondently in front of him.

'Oh, William, what will you do?'

'I'll stay here till midnight – till everyone else is in bed, an' I'll go home then. You'd better be gettin' home now.'

'Oh, William – I couldn't, William. I'll go an' get you something from our house. I'll get you some of Daddy's clothes. Oh, William!'

William, deeply touched, could only stare at her and mutter gratefully, 'Thanks – thanks, he's bigger'n me, but they'll do – *anything'll* do.'

He watched her anxiously through the dusty little window of the summer house as she crept to the hole in the hedge and disappeared. Then he heaved a deep sigh, drew his covering around him, sat down on the summer-house seat and waited.

He was not left in peace for long. The voice which had first broken in upon their desert island sounded again – this time nearer. It was evidently walking round the garden with a sympathetic friend.

'And that wicked girl went to the grocer's and stayed there the *whole* afternoon – it's that young man they've got now – it's always the young men, my dear – that's the worst of girls – and she left the house *entirely* unguarded, my dear – didn't *even* lock the door – and I came back and – yes, my dear, *all* the silver gone from the dining-room – some thief had been in and – oh, yes, I've telephoned the police – and good gracious, the wretch has even taken the tablecloth we had hanging up in the back garden! Did you *ever*?'

'Have you – have you looked in the summer house? He may be hiding there.'

William grew hot and cold, and took up his position immediately behind the door.

'No, my dear and I'm not going to. I don't think it's fair to my friends and relations – I'm not thinking of myself. But – suppose he were there. He's sure to have a revolver. I'd make a fine target for his revolver, silhouetted against the light.'

'Y-yes. But couldn't we get pokers and dash in and stun him before he's time to move?'

William, pressing himself and his tablecloth tightly into the corner, behind the door, was aware of a curious sinking feeling in his insides. Some people, he decided, hadn't any hearts at all.

'I don't think so – we might so easily kill him by mistake.'

'Well, then, at any rate we can lock the door and keep him there till the police come.'

A cold perspiration broke out over William.

'The lock won't work. Do you know, my dear, I'd rather go further away just in case there *is* anyone there. Suppose we go indoors?'

The voices died away in the distance. The tenseness of William's form relaxed. His fixed look of horror and apprehension faded. He ran his fingers through his hair.

'*Crumbs!*' he whispered.

It seemed hours before the door opened and Joan staggered in with a bundle.

'Quick, William darling,' she whispered. 'Put them on, an' we'll go home. No one saw me getting them. I'm 'fraid they'll be a bit big, but we can turn things up.'

Her fear was justified. Mr James Clive, her father, was six foot six in height. On William, his coat nearly touched the ground. His trousers, though rolled up bulkily at the ends till they could be rolled up no more, considerably impeded William's progress.

'Oh, William, they'll do,' she whispered at last. 'They are a bit big, but they'll do.'

William, in Mr Clive's clothes, would have made his fortune on a music-hall stage. Strong men would have wept tears at the sight, but Joan's loyalty was such that only affectionate concern was in the glance she turned on him. William's face was set and determined. He thought that the end of his troubles was in sight, as he rolled the tablecloth into a ball and put it beneath his arm.

'They – they may be able to track us if we leave it here,' he whispered. ' 'Sides, someone's stole my clothes an' I'm jolly well goin' to steal someone's tablecloth.'

The curious couple walked down the road. Joan kept throwing little anxious glances at her companion. He certainly looked very queer. She hadn't realised that the suit would be *quite* so much too big. So far they had not passed a house. Now they were passing a roadside cottage.

A man came out of the cottage and stared at William open-mouthed. Then he leant against the wall, put his hands to his sides and emitted guffaw on guffaw. William merely threw him a murderous glance and proceeded on his way with as much dignity as his trousers allowed him.

'Missus?' called the man, wiping his eyes.

A woman came out, saw William, gave a piercing scream of mirth, and leant helplessly against the wall with the man. Two small children followed and joined in the shrieks of merriment that to William seemed to fill the entire world. Joan put her hand to that part of the long sleeve where she judged William's hand might be, and gave a sympathetic squeeze. Yet even Joan's heart sank at the thought of the journey through the village that lay before them.

The next house they had to pass was the house where Joan lived. To her consternation, Joan saw a figure in a black dress and white apron at the gate. It was too late to turn to flee.

'Well, I never, Miss Joan. Your mother says you're to come in at once. She's in a terrible state over you – where *'ave* you been?'

'I *must* go home with William,' pleaded Joan.

'That you must not,' said the housemaid, taking her hand. 'Your mother said I was to find you and tell you to come in immediate. You've 'ad no tea nor nothin'. As for you,' she turned a devastatingly scornful eye upon William, 'dressin' up an' thinkin' you're so funny – well, you won't get *me* laughin' at you – you oughter be ashamed of yourself.'

With a contemptuous sniff she led away the reluctant Joan. William continued his pilgrimage alone. He went slowly. He went slowly for two reasons. One was that the thought of the journey down the village street filled even William's heart with apprehension. The other was that his trousers were coming unrolled and his hands were so far up the long sleeves of the coat that he could not extricate

A WOMAN CAME OUT, SAW WILLIAM, AND GAVE A PIERCING
SCREAM OF MIRTH. TWO SMALL CHILDREN FOLLOWED
AND JOINED IN THE SHRIEKS OF MERRIMENT.

WILLIAM CERTAINLY LOOKED VERY QUEER. JOAN HADN'T
REALISED THAT THE SUIT WOULD BE *QUITE* SO MUCH
TOO BIG.

them. He was glad that dusk was at last falling. He was aware that a tall figure was approaching from the opposite direction. He shrank into the shadow of the hedge, and hoped that it would pass without observing him. It did not. It stood in front of him, barring his way, and slowly adjusted a monocle. With a sinking heart, William looked up into the face of Joan's father.

'Excuse me, young man,' said that gentleman, 'but either you and I patronise the same tailor and have had identical ideas this spring as to style and material, or – or,' his hand descended firmly and held the back of William's neck, '*or* you are wearing a suit of my clothes, in which case I must ask you to come home with me and take them off.'

He began to impel William gently back towards his house.

'If you'd jus' let me *explain*,' said William, pathetically.

'Explanations,' said Mr Clive, transferring his hold from William's neck to the collar of his coat, 'are tedious, unsatisfactory things. Why trouble yourself with them? I merely ask of you, as one gentleman of another, that you will return to me the garments that you seem to have absent-mindedly appropriated.'

Even William's spirits were crushed by the repeated blows of fate. He did not speak again till he was face to face with his captor in the library of Joan's house, but with Joan nowhere to be seen. He was pale and stern.

'But I've *nothin'* else to wear,' he said, *'nothin'*. You don' want me to go all the way home in *nothin'*?'

'What,' said Mr Clive, 'were you wearing before you purloined my suit?'

'I was wearin' a tablecloth, but—'

'Then I suppose you can go on wearing a tablecloth.'

'But – but you don't want me to go through the village in a *tablecloth*?' said William in frenzied despair.

'You can go through the village in a table napkin for all I care,' said Mr Clive, heartlessly. 'I paid twelve guineas for this suit only last week, and I'm not going to have it mucked up any more. It'll take about six years in a press to take these creases out, anyway. I don't know what mischievous business you've been engaged in today, but I can guess who got hold of this suit for you, and I'll have a few words with Miss Joan on the subject this evening.'

William glared at him savagely.

'Nothin' to do with Joan,' he said. 'I got it myself.' He divested himself of the suit, shook out his tablecloth and wrapped it round him, scowling darkly. 'Well,' he said, slowly and bitterly, 'if you don't mind me goin' through the village in *this*—'

'I don't mind at all,' said Mr Clive pleasantly, 'not at

all. Allow me to see you to the door. Good-night, William.'

He closed the door and went to the library window. There he watched the white-clad figure disappear down the drive. 'That young man's progress through the village,' he said aloud, 'ought to be worth watching.'

William set out once more on his adventurous journey. At the thought of the village street his knees felt quite definitely unsteady. Never to William had his home seemed so near and yet so unattainable. Suddenly he thought of the path over the fields and through the churchyard. It would bring him out a good way beyond his home, but it would avoid that nightmare of the village street.

William climbed over the stile and set off over the fields. It was nearly dark anyway. He could see no one near . . . He climbed the second stile that led into the churchyard, and began to walk forward. Suddenly a woman who had been standing with her back to him, reading one of the gravestones, turned, stared at him with open mouth and eyes, gave a scream that made the hair on William's head stand upright, and shot off like an arrow from a bow, falling head over heels over the opposite stile, picking herself up and running with deafening screams in the direction of the village. William, feeling slightly shaken, sat down behind a tombstone to recover.

Several people passed, but William's nerve had gone. He dared not emerge from his damp and gloomy refuge. At last he heard the sound of many cheerful voices, as if seven or eight people were coming together through the churchyard. His spirits rose. He would tell them his plight. Seven or eight people all together would not be afraid of him . . . He rose from behind his tombstone and with eight wild yells eight young women made for the horizon. All but one. She tripped over a stone and crouched with her head on her hands where she fell. With a thrill of joy William recognised his mother's housemaid. His troubles were at an end. She would fetch him his overcoat.

'Ellen –' he began.

'OO-*ow-ow-ow*!' yelled Ellen.

With a shriek more piercing than he had yet heard, Ellen fled from William's sight.

'I don't know where William is,' said Mrs Brown to her husband. 'He wasn't in to tea.'

'Don't worry yourself about him unduly,' said her husband. 'There was a rumour rife in the village as I came from the station to the effect that William had been seen walking in the direction of the village over an hour ago wearing a suit of clothes of abnormal size.'

Mrs Brown sat down suddenly.

'Abnormal size? But he was wearing his ordinary suit at lunch.'

'I can't explain it,' said her husband. 'I merely repeat the rumour.'

'An hour ago – then why isn't he home?'

'I can't say,' said her husband callously, opening the evening paper.

At this point an unearthly yell broke the silence of the house, and Ellen rushed into the room, flinging herself beneath the table.

'It's come after me,' she screamed. 'It's at the side-door – Oh lor! Oh lor! – It's there, all white an' all. Oh, don't let it get me – I don't want to die – I'll repent – I'll – Oh lor! Oh lor!'

Mr Brown laid down his paper with a sigh.

'What is it?' he said wearily.

'Oh lor! Oh lor!' sobbed Ellen, beneath the table.

A figure appeared in the doorway – a wild figure, with a fierce, indignant, aggrieved expression and hair that stood up round its face, a figure that clutched a ragged tablecloth round it with certain enraged dignity.

'It – it – it's William,' said Mrs Brown.

'But they was *stole* off me,' said William wildly.

'So I gathered from your account,' said Mr Brown, politely.

'Well, is it fair to 'speck me to pay for things wot was stole off me?'

'I have already remarked that if I observed in you any sudden growth of such virtues as cleanliness, tidiness, obedience, silence, modesty – er – and the rest, I might myself contribute a little towards the waistcoat, say, or the collar and tie. We will now consider the discussion closed.'

'It's ever so long past your bedtime, William,' said Mrs Brown. 'Do go to bed. I simply can't bear to see you wearing that dreadful thing any longer.'

With a glance of sorrowful anger at his parents William drew his tablecloth about him and prepared to depart. He felt injured, infuriated, ill-treated, and weary. His self-esteem was cruelly hurt. Screams of laughter came from the next room where his grown-up brother and sister were relating his adventures to a friend.

The telephone rang.

'William, someone wants to speak to you.'

He took the receiver unsmilingly.

'William, Daddy said I could ring you up to say good-night to you. I was so sorry I couldn't go home with you. William, I don't think you looked a bit funny in those things – I think you looked *nice* in the tablecloth and it wasn't your fault – and you were awfully brave about it – and wasn't it *fun* – the desert island part? – I *did* enjoy it – we'll play a game like that again soon, won't we? – Goodnight, William darling.'

'Goodnight.'

William hung up the receiver and went upstairs to bed. He held his untidy carroty head erect. On his freckled face was a softened expression – nearly as good as a smile – he wore his tablecloth with an almost jaunty air.

He was himself again.